CALLOUS

CALLOUS

KEN BRUEN

MYSTERIOUSPRESS.COM

INTEGRATED MEDIA

NEW YORK

This is a work of fiction. Names, characters, places, events, and incidents either are the product of the author's imagination or are used fictitiously. Any resemblance to actual persons, living or dead, businesses, companies, events, or locales is entirely coincidental.

Published in 2021 by MysteriousPress.com/Open Road Integrated Media, Inc.
180 Maiden Lane
New York, NY 10038
www.mysteriouspress.com
www.openroadmedia.com

CALLOUS

Mary Casey, seventy-nine years old, a tough Galway woman.

Her home was her absolute pride.

A small house in Claddagh, one of the rare, precious, coveted original fishermen's cottages. You had to be intimately connected to procure one of these sought-after homes.

Alone in her own home, she was trying to get accustomed to the silence. Her late husband, Tom, would have been proud of her, but then, he most always was.

A fisherman, he had been drowned during the great storm of 2009.

The sea giveth
The sea taketh away.

Another pride of possession was a cross from the penal times, carefully framed in a heavy wood.

A picture of Tom, alongside.

Late on the first evening, she was in the kitchen, having a wee dram of poitín to ease the solitary air.

An almighty crash came from the sitting room.

Not a woman easily spooked, she went to investigate. The frame containing the cross was in three broken pieces on the floor; the cross itself was high on the wall.

Inverted.

She blessed herself.

On the mantel was a photograph of a young woman, Kate Mitchell, her only niece, living in Brooklyn. After Tom passed, she had had what the Irish call a dark premonition, so she'd made a will, leaving her only possession, her home, to the girl.

A faint sound came from upstairs.

Giggling?

No.

Couldn't be.

Kids?

She sat in the kitchen for hours, her rosary beads moving through her frail fingers. But there were no further occurrences and she went to bed, slowly, with a sense of unease.

Midnight, a horrendous scream woke her, Mary sat up, rigid with fear.

A man at the foot of her bed. He said,

"We gave you a chance to move."

He pointed to three huge water bottles, said,

"*Uisce beatha.*" (Holy water)

Mary was discovered two days later, sitting upright in bed, the cross from the beads embedded in her eye.

An autopsy

                    Dismayed the pathologist.

He redid it four times, muttered,

"What in God's name. . . ?"

Reluctantly, very, he gave the results to the Guards, said,

"This is very odd."

The commissioner, cynical in a fashion that passed for banter, said,

"Odd we can handle."

The pathologist thought,

Oh, yeah?

Said,

"She was drowned."

* * *

An American tourist exclaimed,

"Gee, I love Galway in the fall!"

They were having a drink in McSwiggan's, where a tree is growing in the center of the bar (don't even ask; it's an Irish thing, i.e., beyond explanation)

A local, barely concealing his scorn, inquired,

"You mean, 'tis autumn."

The visitor, taken aback, said,

"Yeah, I guess, right."

The local pushed,

"You'd like it a whole lot better if you spoke right."

The visitor turned to his wife, a hardy lady from Salt Lake City, asked,

"Did he just, like, diss me?"

His wife, a diplomat, tried,

"Maybe it's that Irish irony."

She didn't believe that for a second, but as a Mormon, she was experienced in verbal abuse, leaned over to the local, suddenly pinched his cheek, said

"Cheeky devil, aren't you?"

THE IRISH DISMISS HAUNTINGS

AS

TOO MUCH DRINK

OR

NOT ENOUGH

I became a priest
  Because of Naïveté.
  I stopped being a priest
  Because of Despair.
                    If you saw my CV
  It would read like this:
  Ex-priest.
  Ex-cop.
  Ex-ile.
  My father was a cop.
  And one of the 9/11 first responders.
  My mother was Irish.
  A seamstress.
Who works at that anymore, outside of the Eastern sweatshops?
  My sister, Kate, part-time junkie, full-time missing person.
  She was the much-loved niece of her aunt who lived in Galway, and she was heartbroken to learn of this lady's horrible death.
  My dead brother, Patrick, had Down syndrome.
  My elder brother, Colin, was a marine and deployed in Afghanistan.
  I don't believe in ghosts.
  I do believe in hauntings.
  My name is Tommy Mitchell, but I've always been called Mitch. Even in my time as a priest, I was Father Mitch. I was born, raised in Brooklyn, with my mother's heavy emphasis on Ireland riding point.
  Shamrock cushions, stew for Sunday dinner, spuds and

cabbage most every day, John F. Kennedy, interchangeable popes in tired frames on the tired wallpapered walls.

The Clancy Brothers on the turntable.

Irish dancing for my sister, hurling for the boys. The soft *t* barely lurking in our Brooklynese, a tiny lilt in our narrative.

Alongside hurling, we played baseball. Hurling gives you an edge for that, except no Irish sport focuses on throwing the ball so we washed out automatically as pitchers. But boy, I could bat like a banshee.

And did.

My father, he'd been attached to Brooklyn South and his squad was in Manhattan on 9/11 as a team-building exercise. When the North Tower came down and that maelstrom of dust came rushing up the street, people fleeing in terror from it, my dad and his buddies rushed

Into

It.

Years later, he developed the respiratory disease from the gases, fumes, toxic waste, and he and the other responders had their benefits stopped. The heroes were forgotten.

The day we buried him was the day I joined the cops.

Came out of the academy near top of my class, got assigned to a beat in Williamsburg.

I lasted barely a year, my final call-out a domestic, a man was bent over his wife, who was lying on the floor. First, I thought, He's applying CPR.

He wasn't.

Using a blunt tin opener, an old-fashioned one, he had managed to sever most of her head, turned to me, wailed,

"I can't cut through the bone."

I had my Glock out, fired point-blank into his face.

It jammed.

The force had long complained of this weapon being likely to do just that. My partner pulled me away, screaming at me to "Get a grip."

The man got off the floor, sunk the tin opener in my partner's carotid. He bled out in minutes. My Glock worked on the next try and I emptied it into the man.

End of my career.

From a cop to a priest?

I mean

Really?

Like this:

Kate, my beloved sister, recently weaned from heroin, simply disappeared.

Colin, my elder brother, was MIA in Fallujah. Patrick, my Down syndrome younger brother, died of a heart defect and my mother lost the plot.

Utterly.

Spun off into a madness consisting of leprechauns, Jameson, séances, hysteria, and a dark fundamental Catholicism. In one moment of rare clarity, she lamented,

"Oh, Mitch, if only you'd been a priest."

I became a priest.

Madness?

Or perhaps the great Irish tradition of sons joining the priesthood to please mothers who could never truly be appeased

Those days, the hierarchy was having a serious shortage of recruits. The scandals had seriously battered the usual influx of novitiates.

So they literally fast-tracked my, let's be sarcastic and call it *vocation*, and, in jig time I was a curate in the small parish of my neighborhood.

I was a lousy priest.

Lack of belief.

Though that has hardly been much of a stumbling block to the high-flyers in the Church.

Confessions.

They fucked my head entirely.

I felt like I was just killing time as a witness to domestic abuse and, whereas as a cop I could kick the shit out of perpetrators, now I had to suck it up.

I quit.

Told the bishop,

"I quit."

He was outraged, near spat,

"You can't quit, there's a process."

I threw my clerical collar on his huge, adorned desk, said,

"I just did."

My mother said,

"You'll burn in hell."

Maybe.

IN
GALWAY
NO
ONE
CAN
HEAR
YOU
GRIEVE

Diogenes Ortiz
   Styled himself
      As
         A
            Benign
              Thug.
His father was Colombian, and his mother?

Long gone.

He'd been six when he watched his father stab his mom in the eye with the crucifix from her special rosary beads, blessed by Pope John the twenty-third, not that that provenance much helped her, really.

Dad got shit-rich from coca, cocaine.

Sent his only son stateside for education and protection.

Señor Ortiz had most of his business dealings with *the Gentlemen of Cali*, who, despite their description, dispatched his daddy in brutal fashion.

Using the "Colombian necktie," which involves pulling your tongue out and the face pulled back.

           You get the drift.

Diogenes disappeared into the American Midwest soon after.

Resurfaced as an adult, in Galway.

Made his appearance in
       The fall.

September 2019, the month of his mother's anniversary.

Autumn, if you will.

Dio, as he became known, suggested a somewhat down-home boy, mellow even.

Phew-oh.

Nothing could be further from the predatory truth.

In appearance, he cultivated the style of an *ascetic*. Tall, gaunt, bald head, intense burning eyes, dressed always in black, hand-crafted black leather long jacket. Silk T-shirts, black brogues made in London.

He had few passions, but chief were:

Maria Callas.

Philosophy.

Rumor had it he'd studied metaphysics at the Sorbonne, been a brief tutor at Yale, but the most deadly rumor was he'd been embedded with the Zetas.

The Zetas were the most ruthless of all the cartels, possibly the only outfit the cartels feared. Composed of ex-Mexican Special Forces, hardcore mercenaries, they brought ruthlessness to a whole other level.

Whatever the truth in this, it was around this time that Dio enlisted an ex-CIA black-ops guy, name of Keegan.

It was Keegan who introduced Dio to the water gig: pour gallons of water down a victim's throat. Drowning on dry land, he called it.

Dio brought his crucifix-in-the-eye signature to the mix and they joked they almost had a religious form of killing.

Mostly, they enjoyed the combination of the two bizarre methods.

Their plan for Galway was to bring crystal meth to the city, envisaging a megafortune in jig time.

Unknown to Keegan was Dio's other main reason to stay a time in Galway.

Love.

Obsession.

Passion.

For a girl who looked like Maria Callas.

When he and Keegan had first tried by normal means to buy the cottage from Mary, Dio was transfixed by a photo on Mary's mantelpiece.

He gasped in near wonder,

"Is that Maria Callas?"

Mary had scoffed at him in the fashion only a Galway woman can, answered,

"Don't be an eejit, 'tis my gorgeous niece Kate, and if anyone was to get the cottage, t'would be Kate."

Her name was

Kate Mitchell.

Sister of the ex–priest/cop/ile.

Dio had intended staying only long enough in Galway to set up the meth houses, but now a whole new idea blitzed him.

He'd kill the old bitch who called him an eejit, and that had to bring Maria Callas to Galway, where he'd woo her.

As he and Keegan walked away from the old woman, she shouted,

"*Nil aon blain ag fanadh leat!*"

This is difficult to exactly explain in English, but approximately it means,

"You have fuck-all time to live, you shithead."

(It doesn't actually have "fuck" or "shithead," but it gives a nice zing to pretend it so.)

Dio asked Keegan,

"What is she saying?"

Keegan thought,

The fuck would I know? It's Gaelic.

But

Said,

"I think she was sending you an Irish blessing."

Dio stopped, looked at Keegan with his reptile/lizard eyes, warned,

"You're my go-to guy, but don't *ever* . . ."

Pause.

"*Ever* think you can jerk me off."

THEY
    NEVER
        FOUND
            HIS
                HANDS.

—BRADFORD MORROW, *THE FORGERS*

If you were to picture Maria Callas, in her prime, the triumphant years of La Scala, you'd see the haunting eyes, like an intense burn—the long, slim face that Callas had worked so hard to achieve, to be, as she'd prayed, *sylph*-like.

The tiny figure, the days of being fat, overweight, never to be repeated, never.

Her face in half-shadow was truly beautiful.

The specter type of beauty that you know is not going to last, that it holds the sense of death in its luminosity.

Kate was the spit of her.

An uncanny identical twin in Williamsburg, Brooklyn.

Like some cruel psychic joke.

You wanted to seriously piss Kate off, mention the resemblance to *her*.

Kate loved the Ramones, adored the Pixies, the Clash.

But Callas?

Forgeetit (heavy lean on the vowels).

Kate had one real heroine and, in line with her quirky worldview, or skewed, more like, it was a fictional character.

The wonderful Claire DeWitt, private investigator in the trilogy by Sara Gran.

Claire DeWitt, private eye, junkie, mystic, practitioner of all kinds of witchery.

Kate did get clean, mostly, bar the odd line of coke and, like in Sara Gran's novels, she decided to disappear.

To Ireland, where she'd been willed a cottage in Galway.

By her aunt, the late Mary Casey, murdered in the Claddagh.

She arrived in Galway on the sixteenth of September.
The date on which Maria Callas died.

MINNA'S COURT STREET

WAS THE OLD BROOKLYN:

A PLACID AGELESS SURFACE

ALIVE UNDERNEATH

WITH TALK WITH DEALS, WITH

CASUAL INSULTS

ALL WAS TALK

EXCEPT FOR WHAT MATTERED MOST,

WHICH WERE UNSPOKEN UNDERSTANDINGS.

—JONATHAN LETHEM, *MOTHERLESS BROOKLYN*

Keegan was the enforcer for Dio.

His current job was to procure houses to use as meth labs. The thinking was,

Get up to a dozen houses, then if one or more was busted, production still continued. The murder of Mary Casey was just—fuckit—collateral damage.

In a stupendous lack of research, Keegan didn't know Mary Casey was the aunt of Kate Mitchell, the obsession of Dio, but Keegan was nothing if not resourceful. He'd spin it as a dastardly scheme to lure Kate into Dio's orbit.

Keegan was a master of spin—how he'd managed to leave the Zetas alive.

No one walked away from a cartel.

Keegan was blond to his boss's black. He had shaggy hair, a face blasted by sun, a surfer's lean, knotty physique, and could go full minutes without blinking, a vital asset in a man to whom intimidation was survival.

He'd never been on a surfboard but cultivated the dopey surfer-dude persona, even to the point of having a battered, shark-bitten surfboard as center point in his office.

His only reading material was *Savages* by Don Winslow. It had the ultimate surfer dudes, dope, and cartels.

He had a total, almost psychotic, devotion to his boss. Dio had rescued him from a hellhole of a prison cell in Nogales.

His only concern regarding Dio was the lunatic fixation Dio had for Maria Callas, and now Kate Mitchell.

Something in the whole scenario spoke to him of weakness.

Keegan was a heavy-rock headbanger, Guns N' Roses being his go-to band.

He's played their version of

"Sympathy for the Devil"

As he said, with fake mockery,

"To death."

Keegan had been in Galway for a year before Dio arrived, laying the groundwork, recruiting foot soldiers. He especially favored ex-paramilitaries; they shared his ruthlessness.

He focused on acquiring houses close to the water, to the ocean, for shipments to be brought by cargo freighters. He was surprised how many householders sold up without too much of a struggle, maybe as he was prepared to pay over the odds.

Mary Casey was one of the holdouts, so she got murdered.

No biggie.

One other man, named Charlie Fox, proved difficult, told Keegan,

"Go fuck yourself."

OK.

So Keegan set the troops to implement a brief campaign of intimidation: kill his dogs and leave his cat strung up outside the front door.

Basic stuff.

Didn't work.

So then, a mild beating.

Nope.

Wouldn't budge, said,

"Over my dead body." Seriously?

Keegan could arrange that but decided to handle it his own self.

Because

     Because

          He liked it.

Didn't use the water method but opted for mano a mano.

To keep his reflexes sharp.

Did misjudge his opponent

Badly.

And.

Got the shite kicked out of him.

Fox had been a pro boxer.

Four thundering punches laid Keegan flat, ribs definitely broken, the nose too (again!), an eye that was going to be hard black, but, apart from the agony—which was, it must be said, a bastard—it was the shame and anger at having so badly miscalculated.

He put up a hand, trembling, managed,

"Enough, you got me beat."

Fox, triumphant in victory, sneered,

"Limp away, you worthless piece of shite."

Keegan got unsteadily to his feet, woozy, put out his hand, said,

"No hard feelings?"

Fox spat in his face.

Keegan didn't wipe the spittle, let his head hang down as if totally ruined, moved his hand to his back, extracted the long Bowie knife favored by the Zetas, and in one rapid move, gutted Fox like a fish, stood back to escape the torrent of blood, said,

"Nobody, no bollix, spits at me."

Then kicked Fox in the face, said,

"Like I said, no hard feelings."

DERE'S NO GUY

LIVIN'

THAT KNOWS BROOKLYN

BECAUSE IT'D

TAKE A LIFETIME

JUST TO FIND

HIS WAY

AROUND THE FUCKING TOWN

—THOMAS WOLFE,
"ONLY THE DEAD KNOW BROOKLYN"

What do you do when you've washed out of:
The cops?
The priesthood?
You do.
Drugs
And
Jameson.
I was in such a state of despair that I drank Protestant whiskey.
Black Bushmills.
I drowned myself in the Hasid area of Williamsburg. Something about the fundamental neighborhood of Hebrew conversation spoke to the hellfire basis of my Catholicism.
Does that make sense?
Only if you apply Irish logic with Brooklynese riding point.

In
　　The
　　　　Fall

SELDOM WITH THE HEART,

SOMETIMES WITH THE SOUL.

FEW

FALL AT ALL

IN THE DARK.

IN THE FALL,

I FELL

FURTHEST

OF ALL.

—KATE MITCHELL, BROOKLYN DIARY, 2019

Kate came to in a puddle of piss and vomit.

Lifted her head from the mess, groaned, retched, looked 'round, even though it hurt to raise her head.

Gave a tiny sigh of relief. She at least was in her apartment. How she got there was lost. She managed to stand up, grab a near-empty bottle of tequila, swigged delicately from it. It hit her stomach like acid and she threw up again.

Checked her clothes, a Ramones tee, covered in blood? Once-white skinny jeans, covered in grime. Her clutch bag was on the bed. Begging the God she only half-believed in, opened it.

Phew-oh.

Credit cards, MetroCard, many hundred-dollar bills?

Whoa, what?

Ben Franklins?

Christ, was she hooking?

Most days, she came to praying/pleading with a God of torment that she hadn't been raped. This *kind* of money was horror of a whole different kind.

No way was it what her dead dad would have sneered,

The result of honest toil.

She hadn't shot up for nearly a week, and fought the heroin withdrawal sickness with buckets of booze. The ferocious urge to fix now was screaming, *Just a taste.*

Fuck, yeah, sure, and slap-bang to the five-hundred-bucks-a-week monkey. She wept, bitterly.

On her right arm was a tattoo of an angel.

Zadkiel.

Angel of Mercy
Love.
Compassion.
Every time she glanced at it, she snarled,
"Yeah, right!"
Under a small statue of Saint Jude was her rainy-day stash.
Five oxy tabs.
She muttered,
"This is the day."
She lay on the couch, let Gretchen Peters sing softly in her buds, nearly missed the slight plop of mail. She thought,
Bills and threatening letters, final notices on all my appliances, especially my credit card.
When the oxy kicked in and a cloud of bliss enveloped her, she made some coffee, even managed to shuck a cig from a crumpled pack of Camels, she drifted over to the door, picked up a lone envelope.
Irish stamps.
Say what?
Ireland?
WTF?
She poured some more coffee, the oxy really kicking in, settled in her chair, and opened the letter.
"Sweet Jesus," she gasped.
The letter was from a lawyer in Galway, Ireland.
Informing her of the death of her aunt, Mary Casey.
And.
A bequest leaving her the cottage in Claddagh, where her aunt had lived.
She was delighted, amazed, thrilled, and truly stunned.
She ran her fingers along her angel tat, said,
"Thank you, Zak."

She realized this was a second chance. Well, maybe a ninth one, but who was keeping score? She swore, standing like Scarlett O'Hara.

"I'll be better now."

Hmm.

She had a passport, a stack of unexplained money, and no ties. Like, none.

Go!

Her mind screamed.

She would.

She would just up and flee.

Already she felt renewed. So, OK, the oxy helped, but something deeper, a sense of steel hovering over her usual bewildered self.

Her favorite brother, Colin, was due back from deployment in Afghanistan and would be well mind-fucked. She'd write him, offer to share *a little home in the west.*

Colin, born in America of Irish stock, had the completely unrealistic view of Ireland as Nirvana.

So what?

So fuckit.

She'd make it so.

Their last time together, the night before he shipped out, he'd confessed,

"I'm starting to like the killing."

She'd help him heal. By Christ, she would.

She thought of her younger brother Patrick, always present by his absence.

She smiled, if ever there was an *Oirish* thought, that was it. Patrick, with his Down syndrome features, a beacon for bullies, he'd come home from school, asking,

"Sis, what's a Mongol, a retard?"

Colin, always a hothead, tearing out of the house, laying waste to all the shitheads who taunted Patrick.

Mitch, the fucking *saint*.

Colossal pain in the ass, always with the lame,

"Turn the other cheek" shite.

Until.

Yeah, until he spent a year as a beat cop on Park Slope and Williamsburg, then he morphed into a cynical thug. Anger leaking out of his every pore.

Then the asshole became a priest.

For crying out loud.

She'd said to him,

"Gimme a fucking break, *padre*."

Colin, always privy to some secret source of amusement, said to him,

"Couldn't hack it as a marine, huh?"

Dad, dead way too early.

Mom, a crushed, Valiumed wreck after Patrick died.

She often moaned to her own self,

"It's not that I do drugs; it's that I don't do enough of them."

Word.

"I WASN'T SURE EXACTLY WHERE I WAS

OR WHY

BUT SOMETHING SMART AND MEAN TOOK OVER.

SOMETHING THAT I KNEW WOULD KEEP ME

ALIVE.

IF

IF I LET IT."

—CLAIRE DEWITT IN
IN THE INFINITE BACKDROP BY SARA GRAN

"*Ta tu an bas agam,*"

Said my mother.

You are the death of me. As she lay dying.

Gathered around her bed were a priest (not me, as priest); Colin, my marine brother; and me, the object of her dying scorn.

The priest administered the holy oils, which, they say, ease the dying, and give an acceptance, a grace even.

Nope.

Not a chance.

She took Colin's hand in hers, said,

"*Ta tu and mac is fear.*"

You are the best son.

Then she let out the tiniest breath, died. The priest turned to me, said,

"You should be ashamed of yer own self."

I snarled,

"Don't you start."

He had that old Brooklyn spirit. Never walk away from a fight, said,

"You want to say that outside, you heathen?"

Colin, big, sun-blasted from Afghanistan, towering over us, said,

"Much as it would be a kick to see two priests duff it out, maybe now is not the time."

He put an arm on the priest's shoulder, said,

"Let me see you out." Not a request.

* * *

Boerum Hill.

Writers, right? You think Washington Irving, James Feni-more Cooper, but do you think dive bar?

Worse, cop dive bar.

Me 'n' Colin, after the funeral, that's where we ended, because what do you do after a funeral?

Drink and bitch.

It's like tradition. Piss and moan. The bar there is called Al's.

There is no Al.

There's barely a bar.

Shebeen, more like, with Bud and bourbon. Nowt else, save attitude. It's a mean place for mean cops.

Perfect.

Colin was wearing his combat jacket, his master sergeant's stripes, torn off but still legible, barely, like a prayer never answered, a faint echo of what might have been.

He had his army boots, dusted and worn. I had my old barn coat. Once I think it might have passed for leather. Cop pants, cop shoes. I kept thinking I was wearing my clerical collar, the memory of it like a scar.

We looked like bad dudes.

One of us was for real; the other was still in the bleachers.

The place was jammed, a juke hammered out the Pogues, then the Clash, then the Pogues all over. We stood at the ram-shackle bar; the guy behind it was once a Hells Angel, now serving booze to cops.

Go figure.

He kept a sawed-off and a hurley nearby, in plain sight, a sign above them saying,

YOUR CHOICE.

He barked.

"Gents?"

Colin said,

"Boilermakers." What else?

We got behind those, felt the false warmth kick. I noticed a dog-eared paperback in Colin's jacket, asked,

"What you reading?"

Colin fetched it out, handed it over. What was I expecting? To my disgrace, I expected a Spillane, even a Sheldon; shame on me. Saw,

Drive your plow
Over the bones
Of the dead

By Olga Tokarczuk.

Colin did that finger sign to the bar guy, another round, then to me,

"Suckered you, huh?"

I didn't reply. Saw on the dust cover that the author was a Nobel Prize winner. I tried,

"How'd you mean?"

He reached into the top pocket of his jacket, took out rolling leaf and papers, fixed a smoke. The no-smoking rule didn't carry traction in this no-man's territory. He lit up with one of the ol' army-issue Zippos, then, to my astonishment, passed it to the surly bar guy, who muttered,

"Class."

He fast rolled a second, fired up, inhaled deep, and here's the fuck of the thing. I'd half hoped it was for me. Reading my thought, he said,

"You don't serve drinks."

As if that made any sense at all.

Then, indicating the book, he expanded,

"You thought: A grunt, army dumbass, so some tit-and-ass shite."

Before I could protest, he said,

"Army lit, like Tim O'Brien. Being a marine isn't just point and shoot."

He raised his glass, said,

"To the horrors of peace."

I noticed two obvious off-duty cops sending looks our way. One, a burly beer-fucked guy, was muttering darkly to his buddy. I knew it wasn't anything complimentary.

I asked Colin,

"We heard you were MIA for a time."

He shrugged, chugged his drink, said,

"My unit went off radar for a seek-and-massacre gig."

Before I could ask if I even wanted to know, he said,

"I'm going to Ireland."

I went,

"What?"

He gave the tiniest of smiles, not a gesture he had much recent practice with, said,

"Kate surfaced in Galway. Our aunt?"

Pause.

"Died."

Pause.

"Left Kate a cottage. Kate asked me to come visit, maybe even share."

I was hurt, offended, rejected, angry, managed,

"She invited you?"

He shrugged, said,

"Well, buddy, she sure as shit wasn't ever gonna ask you."

Fuck.

I tried,

"Why not?"

He noticed the burly cop heading our way, said,

"She hates you, bro, and six o'clock, we got incoming."

The burly cop approached, all bristling aggression. He noticed Colin's army jacket, stopped, then,

"Thank you for your service, son."

Colin tipped his glass in acknowledgment; the guy looked at me, said,

"Pity about the shit company you're in."

Colin said quietly,

"Dial it down, buddy."

The guy said,

"This garbage got his partner killed, then ran from the force."

Colin sighed, said,

"You need to very discreetly fuck off."

The guy, slightly flustered, tried,

"Got no argument with you, soldier."

Colin turned away; you'd be silly to think he was done.

The guy thought he was done, pushed,

"This cowardly punk needs to leave."

Colin said, almost in a whisper,

"Or what?"

The guy, now all booze macho and stupidity, said,

"Or I'll drag his sorry ass out."

Colin, in a fluid movement, lashed out with the palm of his hand, hitting the guy close to the carotid artery.

There was a moment of pure stillness, then the guy dropped to the floor like the proverbial sack of dumb potatoes. Colin glanced at the guy's crew, asked,

"Any takers?"

No.

We left after another brew, got outside, and I said,

"Jesus, you might have killed the guy."

Colin rolled another cig, said,

"I sure hope so."

Back at the family home, that sounds almost normal, as if we'd been happy there.

Like fuck.

I brewed coffee. We sat at the large wooden table in the kitchen. Patrick's name was gouged in to the wood. I covered it with a coffee mug. It was not a topic either of us could talk about. I asked,

"Is Kate clean?"

He gave me an odd look, almost impossible to read, but it held a hint of menace, said,

"Yeah, she kicked the H, still drinks, but in Ireland, that's almost mandatory."

I gave that some thought, asked,

"You think she might be up to a visit from me?"

He moved the coffee mug, traced Patrick's name with his finger, said,

"No."

Fuck.

He stood up, did one of those neck movements that fit guys like, said,

"Our aunt was murdered; I'm going to find the guy who did it."

I was dancing along the precipice of rage, asked,

"No one told me."

He chuckled, said,

"Bro, it's a family gig, and you?" Trailed off.

I snarled,

"The fuck is that to mean?"

He leaned on the table, his size and intensity were like a storm hovering. He said,

"You were a cop, a priest and, in truth, our family isn't real *hot* on either."

Now I stood, anger leaking all over my face. I snapped, "Dad was a cop."

He laughed.

"I rest my case."

WHEN ALL THIS WAS BAY RIDGE.

HE WAS MASTERFUL, MY FATHER.

HE DIDN'T SAY

WHEN IT WAS WHITE,

OR

WHEN IT WAS IRISH,

OR

EVEN THE RELATIVELY TAME,

WHEN IT WAS SAFE

NO, WHEN ALL THIS WAS BAY RIDGE. AS THOUGH

IT WERE AN ISSUE OF GEOGRAPHY

—TIM MCLOUGHLIN,
"WHEN ALL THIS WAS BAY RIDGE"

Kate Mitchell surveyed her new home in the Claddagh, Galway. She'd arrived a week earlier and was in a shell-shocked state still. The cottage had been vandalized, the utilities shut off. Rain pelted down as if it were personal.

But the locals were friendly.

Most said,

"Sell it, get a nice apartment." Like fuck.

Her determination impressed them and they told her/ helped her with the Utilities

Builders

Cleaners.

One of them said,

"You're the spit of that opera singer."

She smiled through gritted teeth, heard,

"That girl-een had a fine voice."

OK, if it ingratiated her to the neighborhood, she could suck it up.

For now.

She thus learned the use of "–een."

Man-een

Woman-een

Hand-een.

It was used to either diminish or build up a subject or person, to reduce to less fearsome size or even for affection, as in "girl-een."

The Irish version of English took some getting used to.

She hadn't yet mastered the ubiquitous *fierce*.

The weather was *fierce*.

Life could be fierce good or the exact opposite.

Kate settled for winging it, fall back on being American when language failed. A woman said to her,

"We like Americans . . ."

Pause.

"Again."

Whoa, talk about fuckin' loaded! But Kate, no slouch in verbal warfare, said sweetly,

"Oh my, that is such a relief."

Thinking,

Take that, bitch.

You grew up on the streets of Brooklyn, with an Irish mother on point; a passive-aggressive shopkeeper was going to diss you?

Sure.

She went to see her lawyer, a guy in his sixties, all suit and fuss, no class. He offered tea, laughed, corrected, *coffee?*

Kate let a silence hold, to echo how that question sounded. And she let a little hard into her tone, said,

"Could I have coffee without being patronized?"

A beat.

Then he smiled, said,

"Your aunt will never be dead."

After Kate had signed all the deeds, the lawyer sat back, surveyed her with a cold eye, then he said,

"Would you like me to help with the sale of the house?"

She was genuinely shocked, went,

"Sale?"

He did a movement with his mouth which suggested he had a bad taste in there, or even . . .

Even.

That he might be about to spit.

Which would be a very bad move before a woman like Kate. Instead, he cleared his throat, said,

"Young single woman like yerself, take the money, travel, enjoy the freedom."

His face had an expression dangerously close to a leer. Kate said,

"I'm confused. Did I give you the impression I wanted your advice?"

Now he bristled, said,

"Wiser heads, you know."

She said,

"Pity my brother Colin isn't here."

The lawyer felt in control again, smirked,

"He'd be the sensible one?"

Kate stood up, said,

"He's a marine. He'd put you through the window for talking like you have to a woman."

He picked up a pen, said,

"We're done here."

She leaned over, said,

"You're a fierce man-een."

Kate was waiting for an hour in the Guards station until finally a detective summoned her to a small office. He was in his bad mid-forties, going bald, with bloodshot eyes, a reek of stale alcohol seeping from his pores.

His nameplate said *Det. Clarke.*

He looked at Kate with mild distaste, but that might have been due to his hangover. He said,

"Kate Millet?"

She snapped,

"Mitchell, Kate Mitchell."

He stared at his notes, asked,

"You sure? Says Millet here."

He leaned back in his chair, asked,

"What can I do for you?"

She took a deep breath, said,

"My aunt was murdered. I'm wondering what's been done."

He seemed mildly confused, said,

"Done?"

Phew-oh.

She counted to ten and then on the outbreath said,

"Any suspects, any sign of a motive? You know, police stuff."

He took another glance at his notes, then,

"Inquiries are ongoing."

She stood up, snarled,

"So, like nothing, then."

He gave a sly smile, said,

"I'm not at liberty to reveal details of a current investigation."

She said,

"Bite me."

Outside, she fumed, felt the draw of the heroin bliss but shook herself, wanted a kick-ass drink but forced herself to take a long walk. Ended up on Nimmo's Pier.

Gazed out at the ocean, feeling a deep sense of loneliness. Heard footsteps behind her, didn't turn. A man's voice.

"Hope I'm not intruding."

Then he came alongside. He was tall, in his thirties, maybe, bald with sallow skin, dressed all in black, but very expensive clothes. She knew quality, as when you can't afford it, you are keenly aware of it. Just one of life's little fuck-yous.

His accent was part American, part UK English. She gave him the full appraisal, said,

"You look like a crow."

He gave a small smile, said,

"A raven, perhaps."

He put out his hand, manicured hands, but strong, said,

"I'm Dio."

She sighed, said,

"A name as ridiculous as your outfit."

He let that slide, said,

"You are, I believe, Kate Mitchell."

She shot him a look but he countered, fast, said,

"My apologies but this Claddagh is like a village. An American is known."

Something in his tone had a whisper of menace. She said,

"Take a hike, fella."

He gave a delighted smile, said,

"Such spirit de, del corazón."

She put her hands on her hips, spat,

"Try this: fuck off."

Then she noticed in his finely tailored jacket the tip of a paperback, did a double-take.

She'd recognize that book anywhere.

Near shouted,

"Is that a Sara Gran book?"

He took out the book slowly.

Indeed,

Sara Gran.

The very first Claire DeWitt adventure!

Instead of raging anger, she felt a desperate need for a *fix*.

Just shoot up. Don't even try to figure out this weird shit.

He said, with almost a sheepish grin—not that sheepish was anywhere, *ever*, in his genetic code—but he could wing it, kind of,

"I must confess, you are not unknown to me, Kate Mitchell."

You grow up in Brooklyn, survive the streets there as a functioning junkie, very little in this fucked-up world would flatten you.

His words did.

She reeled back and he reached out to catch her. She spat, "Touch me and I'll gut you." He loved that.

Just fucking loved it.

He said,

"Forgive my presumption, but I know we are destined to be together."

She had heard some shit in her time and most of it from her own family, but this *guy*!

I mean, for fuck sakes, was she to have no peace, having traveled across the ocean?

Then,

She made a dreadful mistake.

Understandable to an extent, perhaps, with the stress she was feeling, but in light of the fallout not forgivable. She snapped,

"You better not let my boyfriend hear this shite."

She didn't have a boyfriend, but she had met a man of vague interest. Mike Shaw, an Irish version of a surfer dude, if such a thing even hints at sanity. He ran a sailing school out of the bay adjacent to the Claddagh.

He wore sweaters that would have looked fine in any episode of *Nordic Noir*, very faded jeans, wild scraggy mop of blond hair and, in total contrast, neatly trimmed beard. He liked to smoke spliffs, took the world very much with an air of utter disdain, and seemed to find Kate, as he put it,

"One splendid example of a spirited woman." Who could resist?

So, OK, nothing really *hot* had gone down yet, but it was there, in the air, the fun dance of flirting with a person who made your pulse race.

Dio's face mutated into something very evil, very ugly. He said, very quietly,

"Woman, do not toy with me."

She mistakenly misread this as some degree of capitulation and couldn't resist rubbing his sinister face in it, said,

"Michael is a Viking to your . . ."

Stalled.

Searching for a suitably scurrilous comparison, found, unfortunately,

"Pitiful punk act."

Dio didn't reply, simply rubbed his face with both hands as if she'd spat at him. Then turned, strode away.

A NAKED LUNCH IS NATURAL TO US.

WE EAT REALITY SANDWICHES

BUT ALLEGORIES ARE SO MUCH LETTUCE.

DON'T HIDE THE MADNESS.

—ALLEN GINSBERG, "ON BURROUGHS'S WORK"

Michael Shaw, the man mentioned to Dio by Kate Mitchell, took, as the Irish say,

"*Life aisy* [sic]."

It wasn't that he didn't give a fuck, more that he didn't give *much* of a fuck. His sailing school ticked over, never making a whole shitload of cash but enough to keep him in the essentials.

Beer.

Weed.

Roof over his head.

He'd never been to the States, but his inner voice was all Californian mellow, perhaps due to the sheer amount of dope he smoked. (Ludes he would have appreciated, but his generation missed the whole Quaaludes gig.)

Even his movements suggested a chilled dancer, moving sure but with no great urgency. His favorite expression/ answer to most anything reflected this mindset.

Like this:

"*Ain't no big thing, man.*"

He just didn't take life too seriously.

Life was about to take him deadly seriously.

Saturday nights, Michael liked to tie one on, have some shots with his pints, maybe grab a chicken curry with chips on the walk home.

But first he needed to pee, badly. He was on the Grattan Road, figured he'd slip onto the beach, relieve himself.

He did.

Back on the footpath, a van pulled up, a guy jumped out, slammed his fist into Shaw's gut.

Shaw, stunned, had the insane thought,

Pee police?

Then he was dragged to the van, thrown inside.

He managed to gasp,

"Gotta throw up."

The man who'd hit him said,

"Do, and I'll break your neck."

Minutes later, they pulled up before a dark warehouse and Shaw was dragged inside, tied to a hard-back chair. The man said,

"Feel free to puke now."

Shaw shook his head, trying to focus, trying to figure,

What the fuck is this?

Two men stood before him, literally a clash of light, one dressed all in black, with a shaved head and exuding darkness if such a thing were feasible; the other, blond hair, huge smile of great teeth and a T-shirt that seemed to proclaim

GUNS N' ROSES.

Shaw, who had managed to make light of nearly every event in his life, wanted to ask

"Ebony and ivory?"

But the vibe coming from these guys was anything but mellow; violence seemed to glow and backlight them.

The Guns N' Roses guys said,

"I'm Keegan and this imposing chap is Dio. He's like . . ."

Pause.

"*The Man, El Hombre, El Jefe.*"

Shaw had a temper, not often on show but you didn't run a business in Claddagh by being a guy who rolled over. He said,

"Not much of a man if he has to tie someone to a chair."

Dio rocked on his heels, his machismo, always simmering, took a hit. He snarled,

"What are your intentions to the lady Kate Mitchell?"

Shaw was taken aback, took him a moment to even recall Kate, then he asked, with incredulity leaking over his words,

"The American babe?"

Dio lashed him with

With

Rosary beads?

It hurt. A lot.

Was this some fucked-up priest gig?

Shaw, reeling from the lash, blood already running down his cheek, said,

"Try that shite if my hands were free."

Dio barked at Keegan,

"Free him."

Keegan, unsure, asked,

"Like, seriously?" Dio shot him a look.

So, yeah, seriously.

Shaw, freed, rubbed his hands, asked Dio,

"Ever hear of the hard right?"

Then shot out his right fist, executing a perfect uppercut to Dio's jaw. Dio was lifted clear off his feet, landing flat, heavily on his back. Shaw said,

"Not so much to say now, shithead."

Keegan whistled, said,

"You're, like, seriously fucked, dude."

Shaw faced him, asked,

"So, what you got, asshole?"

Keegan said,

"You have some cojones, dude, but, alas, not going to have them long."

But he kept his hands casually by his sides, his body relaxed. He said,

"Kate Mitchell, you forget about her, maybe we can let this whole dance slide." As if.

Shaw said,

"I barely know her, but now, now I'm kind of keen to spend some time with her."

Keegan said,

"Wrong, wrong response."

Dio, leaning up on one elbow, plunged a long, thin stiletto into the back of Shaw's knee, clean through. Shaw crumpled.

Dio moved toward him, the rosary beads in his hand, put his knee in Shaw's chest, said,

"If thine eye offend me . . ."

Drove the crucifix into Shaw's right eye, twisted it with ferocity, grunting like a crazed animal.

Finished, he stood up, said,

"Retrieve that cross for me."

Keegan thought,

Like fuck.

His time with the Zetas, he'd witnessed

> Women with their entrails spilling out.

> Children hanging from bridges.

And other atrocities that could still bring a shiver to his spine but this, like, seriously?

He tried.

"Haven't you got, like, a stash of those?" Silence.

It was rare to rarest for Keegan to ever, ever, question Dio.

Dio gave Keegan the look; only maybe three times in their fucked relationship had Dio allowed Keegan to see what lay behind those dead eyes. He did now.

It was malevolent, feral, slithering, encompassing every evil you hadn't even conjured. Then it was gone, crawling back to whatever depth it lurked in.

Keegan said,

"I'm on it."

As he knelt, twisting, pulling to get the cross free of the ruined socket, Dio said, "Find me a hill."

"What?"

"A hill above the city."

Keegan couldn't help it, asked,

"We're building something?"

Keegan realized he was asking way too many questions and, phew-oh, Dio had a real hard-on about being quizzed.

He stared at Keegan for one long chilling moment, then intoned,

"I will build a cross to make them shudder, a monolith to show them true awe."

Pause.

"Then I will crucify that treacherous bitch with rusty nails, and her disloyal howls will ring out over this wretched plain."

Not a whole lot of answers to such a scheme, none of them in the realm of sanity. I mean, did you go, "Great idea."

"Just the ticket."

Or,

Simply,

"You mad fucker."

Keegan, always the survivor, said,

"I'll start the search for a hill."

WHY THE GODDESS

WENT TO HELL

AND

WHAT TO EXPECT

NOW

THAT'S SHE RETURNING.

—ROBERT ANTON WILSON, *ISHTAR RISING*

Kate heard of the murder of Michael Shaw on
  Galway Bay FM.
  And she went
  B
      A
          L
              L
                  I
                      S
                          T
                              I
                                  C.
Like, seriously fucking lost it.
Like this:
Smashed her grandmother's Galway crystal goblets.
In Irish lore, that is serious shit.
Just lashed those beautiful babes against the far stone wall
of the kitchen.
She howled like a banshee.
"Yah fuckin motherfuckin' murderous piece of shite."
Then turned to see Raymond Givens leaning against the
jamb of her traditional half door.
An indication of Kate's frame of mind,
(given that she based her life on Claire DeWitt, a fictional
character)
saw a cowboy in her home, leapt to an Elmore Leonard
character, famed in the TV series *Justified,*

and was only disappointed he's not wearing the hat.

He's older than that character but is chewing on a matchstick.

He drawled,

"Sure didn't mean to startle you, ma'am, but you was a little preoccupied venting with that fine crystal."

Hands on hips, fight mode, Kate snarled,

"Who the fuck are you?"

He tipped an imaginary hat, said,

"U.S. Marshal Mason, recently seconded to Homeland Security, and I need to speak to you ASAP."

He then outlined the hunt to nail Dio and how she would play a part, and before she could object, he added,

"Even as we speak, the NYPD have found a pound of heroin in your apartment; that's fifteen years right there. Or you could work for us."

A wave of tiredness hit Kate, she sighed,

"Fix us some kick-ass drinks there, hombre, if you can find any intact glasses."

He settled for two mugs, poured her a healthy dollop of Jameson, asked,

"Ma'am, you got any sipping bourbon?"

She sneered, said,

"You're in Ireland, drink Jameson, and don't even think of asking for ice."

He aimed an imaginary gun, said,

"Loud and clear, ma'am."

Kate got on the other side of her second drink, felt the jolt, felt feisty.

Mason leaned against a bookcase, a fairly sparse case, as Kate had yet to find her way to Charley Byrne's bookstore.

She said to Mason,

"You carry a gun?"

"Yes, ma'am."

She was definitely up for some mind blitzing, asked,

"What's a girl got to do to see it?"

He could play, said,

"Flout the law."

Kate sprang up, rooted in a cupboard, lit a spliff, asked "They rammed a crucifix into Shaw's eye?

"Yes, ma'am."

She felt hot rage spread through her heart, near spat,

"Just like my auntie's?"

"Yes, ma'am."

She rounded on him, snarled,

"You say yes fucking ma'am one more time, I'll find a crucifix for you."

He moved toward her and she fell into his arms and, despite all the regulations, proprieties, and God knows just decency, they made out on the wooden floor like who gives an unholy fuck.

It was hot.

Almost violent.

Loud (very).

And so damn fine, they hit that sucker a few more times.

Eventually, Mason sat up. Whooped,

"Damn, girl."

They say a man begins to lose interest as soon as he scores.

Kate, precarious as usual, wanted him to leave immediately. She said,

In not too bad an imitation of trailer trash—all she lacked was the bubble gum,

"Hon, that was fine. Not the best but not too shoddy, but let's not get all 'Islands in the Stream' on it. You owe me nothing, but the big enchilada here is, you're not the *clingy* type, right?"

Well, Mason felt fucked in every which way he'd not encountered.

Drawing on his best U.S. Marshal's gravity, he said,

"Sit your ass down. I have some things to lay out for you:

"One: Dio is going to kill you. He has already begun building an ugly, gem-encrusted cross to display you on.

"Two: Dio is the biggest meth manufacturer we have seen in a decade, and he is going to flood the west coast of Ireland for starters.

"Three: No matter what we have tried and—trust me, sweet cakes—we have pulled out every trick in the black ops, we got nada.

"Four: For some bizarre reason, he sees you as the incarnation of Maria Callas."

He wiped his brow, looking like he was sitting over the campfire telling the Pilgrims the Indians were en route.

Then he literally put his finger in her face, said,

"We want you to . . ."

Pause.

"How shall I say, *reengage* with him and find a way to steal his phone. It's the one that has all his data and it's made out of solid gold. When we manage to download his files, heck, we might even let you have the gold."

She asked, reasonably enough,

"You guys have a freaking government backing you and you can't freaking steal one lousy phone?"

"Three agents, deeply embedded in his crew, real professionals, failed."

Kate said nothing.

He asked,

"Thoughts?"

She said, very quietly,

"Don't ever call me sweet cakes."

Mason said,

"Get him to trust you, try to think Maria Callas."

Kate laughed, said,

"I already have callous down cold."

He didn't disagree, said,

"If you turn out to be his go-to chick, we're *gold*."

Kate stared at him, said,

"You call women *chicks*? How can you still be single?"

Mason was learning to let most of her barbs slide on by. He said,

"Arianna Huffington's book on Callas is like,"

He took a deep breath, continued,

"The Bible."

Kate, showing as much uninterest as she could, asked,

"Is it on Netflix?"

"WHEN A SHIP

GOES DOWN

IN GALWAY BAY,

OR THE CLADDAGH BASIN,

AS THE WATER HITS THE BOILERS

THE SHIPS SEEM TO GIVE OUT

A LAST GASP OF AIR,

ALMOST LIKE A SIGH.

THEN, IF THERE IS AN EXPLOSION,

BLACK SMOKE BEGINS TO CIRCLE,

THEN RISE UP TO THE SKY.

FISHERMEN CALL IT

The Black Soul
(Fishermen always refer to the perils of the
weather as female and, further, refer to her as being
callous)
Callous has many definitions
In the Oxford Dictionary,
But a Galway fisherman likes best,
A Cold Cunt
He claims no knowledge of Maria Callas"

Ex-cops hear stuff all the time.

My sister, being marginally targeted in not one

But

Two

Fucking murders in Galway.

Jesus wept buckets.

I flew over lickety-split.

I didn't tell her.

She'd have blown me off, fast.

Maybe the ex-cop, even the ex-priest in me, screamed caution.

So I took a week to lie low. Explore the city.

I found a cheap hotel on the Salthill Promenade.

Nearing October, it was cold; very.

So, I found myself in Garavan's Bar most evenings; warm, convivial, very Irish.

Perfect.

Few times, a grizzled old drunk nodded but left it there.

I paid for his drinks some evenings.

He asked,

"You a Yank?"

"Yes, sir."

He mulled on that, then: "You can't afford a coat?"

I told the truth, said,

"I had a priest's coat, but I gave it to homeless guy."

Not impressed.

He muttered,

"Get the poor bollix killed if they know it's a priest's."

Showstopper, that.

A Friday, he left before I did.

God forgive me, I thought,

Good riddance.

Closing time, settling the bar bill, I involuntarily shivered at the weather outside. The barman handed me a parcel. It was heavy and I protested,

"Some mistake."

The guy, tired, asked,

"You the Yank?"

"Yeah?"

Pushed the parcel at me, said,

"Then it's for you. Now, I really got to close."

Outside, cold, I opened the package.

A splendid navy all-weather coat.

It fit like a decent rosary. There was a book in one of the pockets.

The Bird Boys by Lisa Sandlin.

An inscription.

Like this:

> *No excuse being cold*
> *The novel is very fine*
> *Bhi curamach (look it up, yah*

ex-priest)

He signed it with,

> Jack Taylor (ex-cop like yourself).

Not all my cop time was futile; I knew about surveillance.

So.

So, I followed Kate, trying to man up, tell her I'd come to help. Like that would happen.

I stayed in her background, like the one prayer on your beads you never recite. It is called

The fall prayer.

Meaning, if you're down to your last plea, then you are fucked nine ways to hell.

SEEING A BOAT

EXPLODE

IN THE CLADDAGH BASIN,

THE OLD FISHERMAN

WATCHED THE BLACK SMOKE

CURL

AND SPIT DARK

EMBERS

INTO THE NIGHT SKY.

>*"'Tis the Black Soul,"*
>They said.

I was sitting on the prom, my legs hanging over the edge of the path, watching the sea crash in the distance against the rocks. I felt something I rare to rarest experienced.

Peace.

The peace that passes all understanding.

Well, not so much. Let's not go wild, here.

A man walked by, holding what seemed to be a dog's leash but no dog, or none I could see. He was smartly dressed, if not, in fact, the most suitable beach wear.

A smart blue linen suit underneath what my dad used to call a Crombie coat. My dad did not use the description in any flattering sense. He was a street cop, tough as they come and contemptuous of *civilians*.

Alas, he saw his own family as that.

I digress.

A tedious tendency I learned in Theology 901, urged,

Digress on matters of faith.

Of course, with the crew of pedophiles, they moved from digression to disappearance.

The man's shoes were a money shot.

Oxford brogues!

Like an escapee from *Brideshead Revisited*.

He was in his fit late sixties but hale and, who knew, maybe even hearty. I asked,

"Lose your dog?"

He said,

"You're an American?"

In a hostile tone.

I nodded and he snarled,

"Just can't mind yer own fucking business."

Phew-oh.

I shrugged, said,

"Move along, fella."

He considered this, then,

"I don't have a dog."

I was tired of this nonsense, stood up, felt a presence behind me, half turned. A man, wearing beautiful, well-tested cowboy boots, like Eastwood in *High Plains Drifter.*

The dogless man said,

"God bless, and look out for a black collie."

I turned to the man with the fine boots and near fell back as he was the spit of a cowboy:

The boots.

Jeans with a heavy buckle.

Waistcoat.

Black duster coat.

And a face so weather-beaten you could rent out the lines on there.

He flipped open a wallet. It had the badge of a U.S. Marshal. He literally drawled,

"I just fucked your sis."

Showstopper.

I swung with my right hand.

Without seeming to move, his open palm came up, stopped my fist, and with his other hand he delivered a brutal shot to my gut. I was on my knees, puking an Oirish breakfast.

Sausages.

Fried egg.

Mushrooms.

Bacon.

Fried tomatoes.

Black pudding.

It had looked a whole lot better on the plate.

The marshal said,

"Sucker-punch. Surely as a former cop, you'd watch for that."

From farther down the beach, the dogless man shouted,

"Hoi, leave him alone or I'll set my dog on you."

Marshal said,

"My name is Mason and what do you say? Lemme buy you some shots of bourbon, we'll maybe bond, shoot the shit, sound good?"

I was slowly able to stand, managed,

"Fuck you and the horse you must have somewhere."

He threw back his head, gave a full-throated laugh, said,

"I like you. Like your sister, you have cojones."

I touched my stomach and, oh Lord, the pain. Maybe some ribs cracked. Mason said,

"Would you feel better if I said, *Your sister and I made love?*"

He waited but I was still trying not to retch, so he began to stride away, ordered,

"Come on, Mitch, you wanna know what the darn heck is going down."

And fuckit.

I did.

Did want to know.

He led the way to a small pub named, ingeniously, the Prom. It was busy due to the TV having a live sports channel. Stepped up to the bar, a young, pretty woman serving. She asked,

"Get you fellas."

Mason gave her the smile, asked,

"Got Maker's Mark?"

She did.

He ordered two and Buds as point. Then he leaned against the bar, shitkicker pose, looked at me, said,

"That is a fine coat."

My stomach hurt but I managed to get the whiskey down, sipped some Bud, asked,

"What do you want, apart from a serious kick in the face?"

He laughed, said to the woman,

"My buddy here, he's a riot."

Then he took his drink, motioned we should move to a table in the rear. Did that and he swallowed the shot, turned the small glass upside down, tapped on its base, said,

"For the record, your sister jumped me."

I said,

"Well, she's a junkie, so any sex means extraordinarily little to her."

He pondered that, said,

"Whoa, family dysfunction, not my gig."

I waited and he took a deep breath, laid out the whole narrative on Dio, Keegan, and Dio's obsession with Maria Callas, how Kate, might be able to dance the psycho to some serious move that would finish him.

I was horrified, asked,

"She agreed to this?"

Mason laughed, said,

"We left her with little choice."

I wanted to slug him so badly, it *ached*.

He toasted me with the Bud, said,

"Yeah, it's a mind-fuck when you want to lash out and . . ."

Pause.

"Can't."

I said, letting conviction leak over my tone,

"I can wait."

He said,

"Oh . . . oh, how threatening."

I did the hand-signal thing to the bar lady, as in, *Same again.*

Her expression soured; she must prefer the more traditional route of haul yer ass up to the counter.

I thought,

Tough shit.

My mind was jittering with snakes of violence and mayhem. I tried again, asked,

"Why my sister?"

The drinks arrived, the lady pointedly ignoring me, had a mega smile for Mason. She said to him,

"Check the bottom of your glass when you're done."

He drank fast then upturned the glass. A phone number on notepaper on it. He smiled smugly, carefully folded it, said,

"We are dealing with a psycho who is about to flood this country with crystal meth. Important folk in DC have a fond attachment to this land."

I pushed,

"And my sister agreed to do this?"

He lied,

"Jumped at the chance to be a patriot."

He'd already told me she had no choice, so he was full of shite.

He did those neck twists, side to side, that assholes do to demonstrate their fitness, then he gave me a studied look, said,

"You remind me of my dad."

I wanted to smack him until that smugness was beaten down. He said,

"Like you, he was a failure, cut and run, that was his gig, which brings me nicely to the real issue here."

I waited, not expecting anything good. He said,

"You have twenty-four hours to get out of town."

I laughed, said,

"Get real."

He stood, put a rake of euros on the table, said,

"We can't have you sniffing around, generally being a giant pain in the butt."

I stood up, tried,

"And if I don't leave?"

He stared at his fine boots, then said,

"Well then, asshole, you will be in a world of hurt."

And he was gone.

The bar lady came over, clearing the table. I said,

"He's married with four kids."

THERE IS ENDLESS DEBATE

ON THE DIFFERENCE

BETWEEN

A PSYCHOPATH

AND

A SOCIOPATH

BUT

ONE THING IS DEFINITE:

CALLOUS IS SECOND NATURE TO THEM.

Colin Mitchell was built like

A brick shithouse.

That description came from his corps commander.

Big and truly angry, he had the look of the actor Tom Hardy, on steroids.

He loved to fight, wade in there, no rules, and walloping freely. It freed him from the simmering rage he carried like a fever.

His younger brother, Patrick, had Down syndrome and was the target for school bullies, until . . .

Until

Colin showed up.

Mayhem ensued.

Later, when Patrick died, Colin enlisted in the marines and they were glad to have him. The perfect soldier.

Smart, loyal and above all, ferocious.

His commander told him,

"You got brains, kid, you could go to the Naval Academy, be an officer."

Nope.

Not happening.

Colin wanted to be with the grunts, not the brass. But the Marine Corps. Serious intent, baby.

Semper Fi, fucking believe it.

He had a talent for leadership and strategy. Saved his unit from scores of IEDs, uncannily knew how to avoid ambush and had an almost supernatural knack of not only locating snipers but tearing them apart.

You want to be loved by your guys, get the snipers.

He did, every time.

Then, a sniper got him.

His Kevlar vest saved his life, but the shot knocked him on his ass. As he lay, there, he realized the worst had happened.

He got shot.

And he stood up, to the amazement of his crew, he said,

"Bring me that fucker's head!"

And they did.

Literally.

He had been assigned to black ops shortly after and did/ saw some shit that no amount of booze was going to erase.

He deployed three times and then Kate asked him to come to Ireland. She told him of the killings around her so he packed his duffel, flew to her.

The first evening, Kate built a fire. They sat on a raggedy old sofa and made hot toddies, getting nice and slowly drunk, no biggie, just slide on to a better place.

Kate told him everything.

He told her nothing.

He asked,

"You want me to go see this Dio dude?"

She explained about Mason and their scheme to put Kate close to Dio. He mulled that over, said,

"I could kill them all."

He said it lightly

But

He wasn't kidding, not a bit.

* * *

Keegan was sitting in the lounge of the G Hotel. Famed as the hotel frequented by Iain Glen from *Game of Thrones*. Dio's acute paranoia had him constantly on the move,

From apartment

To flat

To sundry hotels.

He certainly had the money.

He had called Keegan, told him,

"Get your ass to the G Hotel."

Keegan had.

It was said the hotel had rooms with a color décor to suit a mood.

Keegan would love to see the room they gave to Dio.

Something black with lurid red splashes, perhaps.

A waitress approached, smile trailing, asked,

"May I get you something?"

Keegan used all his charm, said,

"An Americano would go a treat."

She agreed and hustled to get it.

Keegan was dressed in clean chinos, white shirt, and an Orvis suede jacket. He figured it suggested quiet wealth. He admired the soft leather mocs he'd had since Mexico, not his brawling gear. No, for that he used steel-tipped boots.

Dio emerged from an elevator, dressed in his customary black suit, his brown skin adding to the appearance of trendy undertaker. He strode over to Keegan, slid into the opposite chair as the woman arrived with the coffee. She placed it carefully down, asked Dio,

"Something for you, sir?"

He shook her away.

Keegan felt a slight annoyance, as he had taken a small

shine to her but, as with most things Dio, he let it slide. He owed Dio, owed him big.

But . . .

Dio's increasing crazy shit was wearing thin. And the plan to flood the west of Ireland with meth, well, that was just batshit loco. Keegan took a sip of his coffee, bitter, after kick, perfect.

Dio intoned,

"Her brother has arrived."

Keegan wanted so bad to fuck with him, asked,

"The waitress has a brother?"

But Dio was not of a humorous bent, ever.

Keegan said, trying not to let his scorn leak all over his words,

"Two."

Threw Dio, as was the intention. He frowned, anger flaring, snarled,

"Two? Two the fuck? What do you mean?"

Keegan kept it lean and simple, said,

"Two brothers, one a failed priest, the other one, exmarine, maybe special ops."

Dio stood, near shouted,

"Why are we still sitting? We need to get on this."

Keegan nearly said,

I haven't finished my coffee.

But again.

Not quite the right time.

Keegan decided to act fast, take out one brother, let the other storm around, crying vengeance and other shit, then he'd be ripe for the picking.

Keegan loved the game.

Fuck with the prey for a bit, else it was just business and, in truth, biz sucked.

Keegan followed Colin for two days, established the guy liked to get a coffee, sit on the rocks at the water's edge, dreaming of hot deserts, perhaps.

On the second day, Keegan decided to just go for it.

Dio would have liked for the marine to be brought to the warehouse, use the water and crucifix on him.

Keegan felt that was getting old.

And fuck, slow.

He came up behind the marine, who was staring at the bay, his hands deep in his army jacket, Keegan thought,

Die in his work gear.

He took out the Glock, ratcheted it easily. The marine whirled around, stared at Keegan. If he was surprised, he hid it well. In fact, he seemed to have a small smile.

Too late, Keegan clocked a small boy with a fishing rod, coming along the rocks.

The marine said,

"You didn't do the reconnaissance."

Keegan shot him twice, the marine lifted off the rocks, fell heavily in the water.

Keegan turned to the boy, said,

"Life sucks."

Shot him the face.

Twice.

He liked the number.

THE FISHERMEN OF CONNEMARA BELIEVE

THAT AN ISLAND NOT TO BE FOUND

BY ANY VOYAGE

EXISTS NEAR THEIR SHORE

AND THEY CALL IT THE OTHER COUNTRY.

I learned Colin had been murdered from a news bulletin. It spoke, too, of the child killed nearby. I was shocked to the core. I knew Kate's address and went 'round there, two police cars at the front. A guard blocked me, asked my business, I shouted,

"Family!"

He spoke on his intercom, looked at me a few times, then cut off. He said,

"Ms. Mitchell says her brother is dead."

I tried,

"I'm the other brother."

Sounding weak as piss.

The Guard looked at me for a moment, then said,

"Time to push off now. Don't have me make you."

Make you!

I counted to ten, said,

"Here is the address of the hotel I'm at if she wants to talk."

He took the card, put it in his tunic, said,

"You don't want to become a nuisance."

There are many replies to this challenge, but none are wise unless you're armed.

I heard an American had been wounded and a young boy murdered in Salthill.

I learned it from the most reliable source in Irish life.

A barman.

Did I worry about the amount of time I was spending in pubs?

A little.

I was at the counter in Garavan's center city pub, working on a finely drawn pint. The barman, making chat, said,

"They tried to kill a Yank. Any relation?"

                 There are so many horrors in that sentence.

I went,

"Not really."

He gave a shrug, said,

"Now, if you were in France, you'd know they flat-out hate you but in Ireland, 'tis always a little up in the air how we feel, unless we have relatives working stateside, then 'tis no contest, we like you. What can I get you?"

I ordered a double Jameson, saw a slight hesitation on the barman's part, but he delivered, said,

"On the house."

I raised the shot glass, toasted,

"Here's to family."

I finally came across Kate in a place she might not instantly hand me my ass.

A pub.

Neachtain's. Beloved of

Poets

Would-be poets.

Once-were poets.

Not a book published among the lot of them.

But talk.

You got it, yards of horseshit, poetically woven.

In an eavesdropped conversation you'd hear

Ginsberg.

T. S. Eliot.

Never Seamus Heaney because

Duh, he, like, major sold out.

It was vaguely amusing in a shoot-me-now kind of fashion.

Then I saw Kate.

She was sitting with a young woman, and they were deep in conversation. Kate looked wild, sad, beaten/defeated, or just Kate.

The ex-junkie.

Does that sound harsh?

You fuckin' betcha.

The other woman missed being beautiful by about a centimeter, nose too prominent and a mouth that turned down. If the mouth turns down, run.

I approached, tried,

"Kate?"

Lame, huh?

She looked up, flinched, said,

"So?"

I thought,

It's going well so far.

What I said was,

"Can I get you girls a drink?"

Well, fuck me, I was on fire.

Kate stood, said,

"No need, I'm getting another round . . ."

Pause.

"For us."

She headed for the bar. The woman said,

"I think you get to buy your own drink."

I said,

"I guess."

Like I said,

On bloody fire.

The woman said,

"You're an American."

Indeed.

Before I could reply, she asked,

"Marry me?"

I stared at her, so she continued,

"It's not like you're my type, God forbid, but I want that green card."

I went and ordered a large Jameson, gulped it down, and the bar guy drew me a slow pint, said,

"How we do it here."

I nodded as if I understood. I was beginning to grasp that the Irish love talk, no matter if it's relevant, just fill that silence. I turned 'round and the woman motioned me over, said,

"Grab a seat. Kate takes ages to get drinks."

I did.

She had her hair tied back in that serious ponytail women can do without effort, and a T-shirt with the logo over her chest that proclaimed

NOT MY PROBLEM.

She said,

"I'm Nora B."

I hazarded,

"For Nora Barnacle?"

She looked at me with utter disdain, said,

"For bitch."

And for some bizarre reason, she twitched her arm. I saw a tattoo run the length of it: an angel or, rather, let me lean on my clerical schooling, short as it was,

An archangel.

She seemed delighted with what she thought was my shock.

Lest she think she was running the whole gig, I decided to fuck with her, asked,

"How much would you give me if I knew the name of that angel?"

She leaned over, not quite in my face but hovering, sneered,

"I'll pay for your night's drinking."

We shook on it, she spitting on her palm in an exaggerated gesture. Despite this, her hand was cool, a nice feel.

"So . . ."

She said.

"Spill."

I drank half my pint, began,

"It's Archangel Jophiel, patron saint of artists, inspiration for creative minds, and his color is yellow gold, like the middle part of your arm art."

She said nothing for a moment, then,

"Holy shit."

Kate returned with a tray of drinks, said,

"I'm feeling a bit drunk, so I mistakenly bought you one."

This was aimed at me.

"A bottle of non-alcoholic beer."

The greatest insult to a drinker there is, like, decaf coffee; what's the fucking point?

I said, indicating my pint,

"I'm good, thanks."

She stood back, hands on hips, eyes afire with rage. She echoed,

"*Good?* Of all the shite you were, good was never, ever, a part of it."

Nora said,

"Whoa, what am I missing here, you know each other?"

Kate glared at her, said,

"Duh."

I said,

"We're related through drink."

Kate grabbed a jacket from the back of her chair, said to Nora,

"Let's bounce."

The jacket?

I said,

"That's Colin's army one."

She shook the jacket and pushed her fingers through two holes, said,

"He had a book in his jacket and it took the brunt of the shots. He is still in ICU if you cared."

Jesus, I nearly asked her the title of the book. Fuck me.

Nora, looking a blend of . . .

Shock.

Dismay.

Uncertainty.

Said,

"I think I'll hang a bit, do some more shots."

Kate spun on her boots, stormed out. I tried,

"She means well."

Nora laughed, said,

"Like fuck."

We drank a lot of tequila, to such an extent that the bar guy handed me the empty bottle, said,

"You killed it."

We staggered to the end of Quay Street, laughing at some obscure lines from *Better Call Saul*.

A squad car pulled up and Nora went,

"Uh-uh."

Two seriously big guards, one looking like a very battered Russell Crowe, barked at me.

"You're Mitchell, the American."

I nodded, not trusting my voice.

He continued,

"Get in the car, we need you to assist in the shooting of your brother.

Nora, instantly sober, said,

"Whoa, not so fast, Sherlock. Mr. Mitchell here has a solid alibi when his brother was shot, and as to who did it, that's your job."

Crowe looked at his partner, who shuffled, then went,

"We'll need to check that alibi."

Nora smiled, said,

"Me. He was fucking my brains out at the time."

ON A MAN WHO DEVELOPED THE SO-CALLED PER-

FECT BODY.

MY BIGGEST SURPRISE IS THAT I DON'T FIND HIM

SEXY.

AS MY FRIEND SERENATA

QUIPS ABOUT SUCH A CHARACTER,

ONE SIMPLY DIDN'T HANKER TO FUCK A MAN WHO DESIRED HIMSELF

—LIONEL SHRIVER, *THE MOTION OF THE BODY THROUGH SPACE*

Close to the old docklands, there is what appears to be a huge gray container.

If you were to have a closer look, you'd realize it's been converted into some kind of office/living space.

That's as much as you'd see due to two burly security guards with savage mastiffs straining on their chain leashes.

The Block, as it's been nicknamed, was once home/recording studio to a band named

Callous

The band had some minor hits, then descended into diva hysterics.

Dio was the current tenant and he'd tricked it out to resemble Hitler's lair.

Why?

Because he was a fucking psychopath.

A large swastika flag lined one wall, and the other had a massive mural of Maria Callas. He had all her recordings lovingly built into a steel case. Touch those and lose your freaking hand, for openers.

Dio was presently in a torrent of bile and rage, directed at Keegan.

A large German shepherd lay in front of a blazing fire with its eyes following Dio. The dog, of course, was named Blondie.

A small framed photo of Kate Mitchell stood beside the air mattress Dio infrequently used. In his madness, he'd lovingly written with a Sharpie,

To the love of my life from Kate

Dio roared at Keegan,

"You fucked up double. You failed to kill the marine, and the other brother is strolling around without a care in the world."

Keegan tried to explain.

Dio nearly grabbed him, but even Dio in his most monstrous episodes knew better than to lay a hand on his second in command. They had been together a long time, endured all kinds of weird and wonderful events, but there was a side of Keegan that Dio had never seen. He knew it was there, and, so far, he hadn't crossed that unknown line.

Dio was dressed in an all-white karate outfit, but he had never studied the art. He just liked the feel of the garment and it gave the impression(maybe) that he had karate skills.

Keegan, as usual, was in his semi-biker mode. Black battered leathers, with a Hells Angels badge on the front, a chapter out of Oakland. Those you didn't pretend to have—those you got with blood.

He had boots with steel-toe caps and inside the jacket he carried a Blackhawk Magnum. These suckers weighed a ton but seemed to fit smoothly with the lie and fall of the leather jacket.

Keegan took Dio's tongue lashing in stride, stood rock-still, no expression.

Dio demanded,

"What are you planning to do about this now?"

Keegan seemed to give it serious consideration, then said,

"Nothing."

Dio thought at first he'd misheard. Nobody said

No

Or

Nothing

To him,

And was still around.

Keegan had been the one constant, the fixed loyalty, utter devotedness.

But,

And here was a big but,

Lately, cracks were showing in their way of handling things. Keegan was more than vocal in his disapproval of the whole meth plan, had even gone on to say,

"Patron, we have mountains of cash; let's chill, enjoy it."

This, a sentence fraught with peril.

Dio picked up a heavy black rosary. It seemed to fall forward with sheer weight on the solid gold cross. He fingered the beads like a garotte.

He stared at Keegan, who by ill luck or just dazedness had a T-shirt that said

Guns

N

Rosaries.

Dio said in, a quiet, measured tone,

"You were sent on a simple assignment: shoot the American brothers. But what do you do?"

Keegan said nothing, feeling Dio was about to lay it out.

He did.

Like this.

"*You shoot the marine with most powerful handgun on the planet, and he lives.*

"*Lives!*

"*And the other brother, un-fucking-touched, is strutting 'round the city getting liquored up and screwing the local gals.*

"*Lest any of the above escape the cops, you gild the fucking gig by killing a five-year-old kid.*"

Keegan felt a nigh-unyielding urge to slap Dio, hard and fast across the face. Just drop the fucker. He said,

"I'll finish the job by the end of the week."

Dio swirled 'round to face the portrait of Maria Callas, implored,

"Get me some decent help, my darling."

More and more, Dio was talking to the portrait, and this was becoming a liability. Keegan had no problem with madness/craziness in a boss. Most times it was actually a bonus, but this shit?

He ran a Guns N' Roses song in his head, and it is nigh impossible to get that tone of menace without the band screeching wild on a stage.

Dio now said,

"Kill the brother who is still walking around and kill him today, then you might . . ."

Pause.

"Might."

Pause.

"Be on my cool list again."

Then he waved a hand in dismissal.

Keegan thought how fine it would be to slash that hand with his well-worn machete.

Mason had an edge he didn't share with Kate Mitchell.

An informant.

A rat.

An asset?

A snitch.

What-the fuck-ever.

It was getting him the juice on Dio and precisely how nuts Dio was becoming.

Mason had suggested they meet in McSwiggan's. Where

else do you get a tree growing in the center of the bar? Mason was lingering over a pint. He'd noticed that these pints of dark fire were giving him a pot. Fuck, a U.S. Marshal couldn't have a beer belly.

He did ask the bar guy,

"You got any, like, Guinness Lite?"

The bar guy gave him the look, said,

"They tried it a few years ago."

His tone suggested he'd rarely encountered such idiocy. Irish contempt works on two levels: you feel as if you got a pat on the head and a shoe in the hole.

Mason, still feeling the glow, asked,

"How'd that work out?"

The bar guy leaned back, asked,

"How'd that New Coke go?"

Touché.

Mason had half the pint gone when his snitch arrived, looking furtive.

He spotted Mason, strolled over as if this were no biggie.

Mason said,

"How's it going, Keegan?"

Keegan immediately hit panic, snarled,

"Stop using my fucking name."

Mason was amused. Here was the right-hand man to America's most wanted, and his own name spooked him.

Mason said,

"How are things at the meth factory?"

Keegan was sweating, said,

"We've got a problem; I'm supposed to off the two brothers *today.*"

Mason said,

"No problem, use a Glock; it's mostly reliable."

Keegan hated Mason, hated that he was at this fucker's beck and call. A year ago, he'd been swept up in a major DEA bust, threatened with twenty in supermax.

Or

Join the home team.

A straightforward deal.

Fuck Dio, and the charges disappeared.

Mason decided to ease up, said,

"Colin, the shot brother, is well protected, and we'll grab the ex-priest, keep him for a few days."

Keegan, a bigger-picture kind of guy, asked,

"You fucking think my boss will buy that?"

Mason smiled, asked,

"You got a better idea?"

SOME PSYCHIATRISTS CALL YOU *WHISPERERS*

BECAUSE OF YOUR ABILITY TO IMPRESS WEAKER

PERSONALITIES.

I PREFER TO CALL YOU WOLVES. WOLVES ACT IN

PACKS.

EVERY PACK HAS A LEADER, AND THE OTHER

WOLVES

HUNT FOR HIM.

—DONATO CARRISSI, *THE WHISPERER*

I finally got to see Colin in the hospital. He was sitting up in bed with swaths of bandages 'round his chest. I brought some magazines, grapes, and a fifth of bourbon in a Coke bottle.

He was still tan from his deployments and had the nurse in a tizzy.

He said,

"What took you so long?"

I said,

"I was assisting the Guards in their inquiries."

I handed over the stuff, said,

"You might want to go easy on the Coke; it's sipping whiskey."

He took the top off, drank deep, then let out a deep breath, muttered,

"Ah."

Thank God for bourbon.

He accused,

"'Tis not Jameson?"

Indeed.

Very little was.

I said,

"I thought you might like something with a serious kick."

He gave a cynical smile, said,

"You obviously haven't drunk enough of it."

I tried,

"How are you doing?"

He laughed, said,

"I've been shot twice, had to be dragged from the ocean, how would you be?"

"Dead."

The nurse came in, did that number with pillows to prove she did graduate from nurse school. She gave me a sour look, asked,

"Who are you?"

I said.

"His brother."

She was scandalized, snarled,

"And 'tis only now you came to visit?"

Colin was smiling broadly, but then he did have a shotgun of bourbon ingested.

He said to the nurse,

"My brother here was a priest."

Was!

Oh, one of the worst things you could say to an Irish woman. She near spat.

"And what did they fling you out for?"

Like it was her business?

I mean, fuck off.

I said,

"I resigned."

Nope, it didn't get me any slack. She said,

"No wonder the world is fecked."

She bounced away, trailing reprimand.

I asked Colin,

"Do you know who shot you, or even why?"

Colin gave that enigmatic smile, the one that signaled mayhem was stirring, said,

"Not yet."

I pushed,

"Why do you think he shot you?"

He said,

"It's to do with Kate."

Kate?

"Why do you think that?"

He sighed, said,

"Everything's to do with Kate, sooner or later."

I was running out of chat and he was distinctly comfortable with that.

Finally, I asked,

"The book that took the bullets, that saved your life, what was it?"

He was quiet, then said almost sheepishly,

"The Bible."

I didn't really have a response, so he reached in his locker, took out the Bible, handed it to me. It was the King James version and looked a lot like the one my mother used, save for the two large bulletholes. I said lamely,

"Wow."

Colin laughed, said,

"Try to stem that torrent of comment."

This happened a lot in my encounters with Colin. Truth was, I didn't really know how to talk with him.

He was cynical.

Aggressive.

Humorous.

Combative.

And

I could never figure out which it was, or just a mash of them all but, primarily, it was a ball buster. Kate had the same DNA, so they never stopped yapping.

To each other.

To me?

Not so much.

Did it bother me?

You fucking betcha.

Add the relationship they had had with my deceased brother, Patrick, which I never had.

I was the dark sheep in a darker family.

Colin drained the bourbon, belched, sighed,

"Fuck, that was heaven."

I asked as I prepared to leave,

"Anything you need next time I visit?"

He looked at me, said,

"A little warmth."

"You mean like sweaters?"

"No."

He said,

"I mean in attitude. You're a cold fish."

In the corridor I met a priest. He stopped, asked,

"Are you the American's brother, the ex-priest?"

I said,

"I'm a cold fish."

And felt cold with it.

Nora B was waiting outside for me, dressed like Annie Hall, which was a look she rocked. She was leaning on a very battered Porsche.

She asked,

"How'd it go?"

I gave her a malicious smile, said,

"We bonded and hugged."

She said,

"Like that, huh?"

I was staring at the car as I realized she was holding keys. She went,

"Wanna go for a ride?"

I was incredulous, asked,

"In this?"

She laughed, said,

"Unless you have transport."

Maybe she stole it. There was a streak of wildness in her that tottered on plain madness, else why was she bestie to Kate? Kate only hung with the marginally unhinged. She gave a dramatic sigh, said,

"Time to fess up. I have a shitload of money."

Her tone was mock penitent, so I asked,

"Is that a crime?"

She tossed me the keys, said,

"Only if you don't spend it."

Driving that car was like a kiss from heaven. Took me a while to adjust the gears, but then it just flowed. I opened her up when we hit the stretch after the town's limit. I drove for maybe half an hour, the adrenaline blazing through me. Pulled up at a layby, turned the engine off.

Reluctantly, I handed back the keys, stood outside the car, said,

"That was intense."

She smiled, asked,

"Something you might get used to?"

I couldn't quite figure what her game was. I was flattered but suspicious, asked,

"What's your game?"

She was delighted, said,

"It's kind of hot to be fucking a priest."
Sigh.
I said, holding my tone,
"Ex-priest."
She couldn't care less, asked,
"What do you do now that you're not priesting?"
I said,
"Trying to find who shot Colin and maybe even why."
She said,
"Duh."
I echoed,
"Duh? What's that mean?"
"Money."
She said,
"It's always about money."

IN THE SPRING OF 1979,

THE ASHES OF MARIA CALLAS WERE CEREMONI-

ALLY

SCATTERED IN THE AEGEAN.

"HOW SHALL WE BURY YOU WHEN IT'S OVER?"

THEY ASKED SOCRATES JUST BEFORE HE DIED.

"ANY WAY YOU LIKE,

IF

YOU CAN CATCH ME."

MARIA'S ASHES WERE LOST IN THE SEA SHE LOVED.

SHE LIVES ON, LIKE EVERY GREAT SPIRIT,

FOREVER

ELUDING OUR GRASP.

—ARIANNA HUFFINGTON, *MARIA CALLAS*

Kate loved to dance and, due to a nun from Brazil, she'd learned to salsa.

Kate adored that full, loose freedom it gave you.

Dio was a dancer, could do a tango to make you almost forget this guy was a stone psycho.

Almost.

Keegan didn't dance, ever. You follow Guns N' Roses, are you gonna dance?

At a Roses concert, you rioted.

Kate was swirling round the floor of the salsa club in Dominic Street

And

Near collided with Dio. He caught her from falling.

This *incident* had been choreographed by Mason. Took four nights until Dio showed up.

She managed,

"*Muchas gracias, señor.*"

He gave his wolf smile, asked,

"*Habla español, bonita?*"

She stood back from him, noticed his sleek black pants and silk shirt, said,

"That was it, well that and *puta.*"

Dio, in a rare moment of levity, said,

"Probably all you need."

Kate smiled. The dude had some moves. He extended a hand, invited,

"Come drink some Champagne"

Dio, like most psychopaths, could turn on the charm and he did so then with nigh ferocity. Kate was more accustomed to the Brooklyn form of romance, which involved a six-pack and the backseat of a Corvette—better if the car was stolen to add to the weak vibe.

Dio ordered a second bottle of Dom Pérignon, turned to Kate, said,

"I must apologize for my crass behavior the first time we met."

Kate was torn between flinging the glass of bubbly in his face or beginning the charade of seducing him, not that she'd have to work that; the guy was well hooked.

She gave him her best smile, said,

"Dancers get forgiven."

End of the evening, he said,

"My driver will take you home and, if I may, invite you for dinner some evening."

She was dismayed, her head full of the schemes she'd been ready to roll out. This etiquette threw her.

The driver was a blond guy, wearing a Guns N' Roses T-shirt.

The car was a sleek gray Mercedes, and the driver held the door for her.

As the car pulled away, Dio blew her a kiss. Keegan, turning the car toward the Spanish Arch, said,

"You made a fine conquest there."

Kate caught his eyes in the mirror, said,

"Best if the help doesn't speak."

Keegan wondered if he was still to procure a cross for Dio to literally nail her but the energy seemed to have altered.

Keegan drove fast and nigh furious to her home, turned off the engine, said to her,

"This is you, right?"

Kate, riding the buzz of the Champagne, still had wit enough to ask,

"How do you know where I live? That's a little creepy."

Keegan, without turning to face her, said,

"That's my gig, knowing shit."

Kate had no reply to this, 'least nothing that would exclude many expletives. Keegan said,

"I'm sorry to hear your brother was shot."

His tone was mock contrite, and he still hadn't turned to face her. She asked,

"What have you heard?"

Keegan rolled a joint, cracked a window, said,

"I heard the shooter wouldn't fuck up the next time."

She was stone sober now, pushed,

"Give me a name."

He laughed, drew long on the spliff, said,

"This is good dope."

Kate got out of the car, stood at Keegan's window, said,

"Your boss likes me; bear that in mind."

Keegan flicked the end of the spliff past her, put the car in gear, said,

"He likes you *now* and, trust me girlie, that can change in a New York minute."

He burned rubber, making a turn, and Kate gave him the finger.

It seemed woefully lame.

WHEN ANYONE ASKS ME

ABOUT THE IRISH CHARACTER,

I SAY, LOOK AT THE TREES.

MAIMED,

STARK AND MISSHAPEN,

BUT FEROCIOUSLY TENACIOUS.

—EDNA O'BRIEN

Dio's plan to flood the country with meth was nearly over before it began. Seven houses had been set up and were preparing for shipment when the DEA hit them.

Twelve men arrested.

None of them Irish, which was a relief to the local authorities. Tracking who owned the houses led to a series of shell companies with a base in the Caymans.

Dio had insulated his own name, which kept him from being identified.

But he was mightily pissed.

Dio had another apartment in Ocean Towers, right across from Galway Bay. The view meant nothing. He didn't ever look at it; his only motivation was power/money.

He had summoned Keegan there after the raids. He was dressed in just sweatpants, his torso covered in sweat and scars. Dio didn't so much work out as endure a grueling fitness regimen.

Keegan was dressed in Guns N' Roses T-shirt from 2001, a bad year for the band and now looking like a real bad day for Keegan.

Dio asked softly,

"How many houses did we lose?"

Keegan preferred it when his boss acted out.

The roaring.

Spitting.

Screaming.

But the quiet tone, fuck, that was unbelievably bad news.

Very.

Dio asked in a near whisper,

"How many houses did we lose?"

Dio looked at his own hand, then with the other began to crack the knuckles, managing to make the action both sinister and threatening, asked,

"How did we lose them?"

Fuck.

Keegan knew exactly *how*. He'd called Mason the week before. He moved back a step from Dio, whose mouth was showing traces of spittle, which was usually the beginning of annihilation for some poor bastard.

Keegan said,

"There is a German guy, one of the chemists, who has been inciting the others to demand more money."

Keegan knew this was a deadly move, but he was truly between a hard place and Dio. Dio said,

"Burn him."

He meant that literally.

Later that evening a man would be discovered in a burned-out Audi. The car and occupant were eventually identified as German.

Three more houses went down. Ireland's CAB, the criminal assets bureau, led these raids with the U.S. DEA as backup.

Dio was, as the Irish say,

"Spitting iron."

It is a stage beyond rage, with brutality riding point. Dio grabbed Keegan by the shoulders, shook him, screamed,

"What the fuck is going down?"

Keegan was almost tempted to say,

"Going down?" The fucking houses are.

Keegan was not the kind of man that people put their hands on, at least not twice. The first guy who touched him he stabbed in the throat. That was in New Mexico, what Keegan saw as their glory days.

Now fading fast.

Dio intuited something in the energy between them, let go of Keegan, sneered,

"So, what do we do? Burn more Germans?"

Keegan was not a fan of that race, as he'd been in a jail in Frankfurt for a time. Clean though; an exceptionally clean jail.

Brutal too.

But if there was one single thing in the crazy world that Keegan understood, it was brutality.

He said to Dio,

"Might be time to move the caravan, hitch our goods to somewhere the officials we buy stay bought."

Dio, never a fool, hated to admit that it made sense, his success to date having relied heavily on his ability to disappear at a moment's notice. His gold-plated cell phone contained everything he needed.

He gave Keegan a friendly tap on the shoulder, Keegan didn't flinch, though his blood did boil. Dio said,

"OK, let's begin a wrap-up, but first I have to crucify that Mitchell bitch."

Keegan was on for that. Be glad to see that *puta* howl.

But.

They both knew Dio wasn't quite ready to quit on Kate/ Maria Callas just yet. He said,

"I'll dance with her a little longer, then the cross."

Keegan thought,

Yah weak fuck.

Said,
"Good thinking."
Dio stared at him, asked,
"Don't you have two brothers to kill?"
Indeed.

IT IS SAID

THAT, AT THE NUREMBERG TRIALS,

BEFORE THE HANGINGS BEGAN,

ONE OF THE TOP NAZIS WAS ASKED,

"HOW DO YOU FEEL ABOUT

THE EVIL

YOU SPREAD?"

THE ACCUSED THOUGHT ABOUT HIS REPLY

FOR WHAT SEEMED

AN INORDINATE TIME,

THEN SAID

"WE MAY HAVE BEEN A LITTLE . . ."

PAUSE.

"CALLOUS."

I was just leaving Garavan's when the bar guy cautioned,

"Be safe."

Perhaps because of my brother being shot, or maybe he simply cared.

I pulled up the collar of my Garda coat, turned into Buttermilk Lane when two men fast approached. The first one stopped, hit me in the face with a crowbar.

I fell back against a wall when the second one snarled,

"Keegan said to cut his throat."

Two thoughts flashed as my face burned in agony:

Who the fuck is Keegan?

But, of more urgency, the statement,

Cut his throat.

What?

My throat?

The first guy pinned me to the ground and the second guy produced a long machete (they had machetes in Galway?).

He was in mid-swing when something crashed into his skull. The second guy went,

"What the fuck?"

The same object walloped him in the throat and then his knees. He was out of the game.

A skinhead stood over me, brandishing said object, a hurley. He put a hand out, said,

"We better skedaddle."

Who says that outside of a Mickey Spillane novel?

I got to my feet and the skinhead gave me a supporting arm. I asked,

"They have skinheads in Galway?"

If I know anything about skinheads, and I knew precious little, it is that the shoelaces on their Doc Martens signify something.

If they had red laces, they had killed somebody.

I managed to look down despite the nausea caused by my for-sure-broken nose, saw,

Red laces.

He said,

"I've a van at the end of the lane."

Sure enough, a white van (aren't they always white vans?). Despite the agony of my face, on the side I could read,

TEMP

DELIVERIES.

I asked,

"Is it stolen?"

He nearly let go of my shoulder, indignation writ large, said,

"It's mine. I paid good cash money for that."

I was too weary to apologize, gave him directions to my new apartment, and he got me lying down in the back of the van and we took off.

We got there and he helped me into my living room. The apartment was small: one sitting room, kitchenette, and a bathroom you could barely swing a skinhead in. A bookcase with three books, a sofa, and two hardback chairs; a beer case served as a table.

He asked,

"You're poor?"

With bewildered tone, he asked,

"You're poor?"

"No."

I sighed,

"It's Zen."

He gave a short, sharp laugh, said,

"I know poor, and this is poverty."

Maybe.

My clerical training kicked into mock whisper:

"Blessed are the poor in spirit."

Fuck that.

I managed to get to the sofa, sit, and commended him.

"There's brandy in the press. Fill a glass and, when I faint, bring it to me."

He was worried, tried,

"You're faint?"

How big a surprise could that be? A crowbar had been smashed into my face.

I said,

"I'm going to fix my nose and, believe me, the maneuver will knock me on my ass."

Nervous, he got the brandy and I did admire him for sneak-slugging a healthy shot. He waited as I put my hands to my nose, one to the side where it was out of line, the other I slammed into the first one and fell of the sofa in utter agony.

"The brandy,"

I croaked.

He knelt, gave me the bottle, and I hit that pain with a dose of brandy, nearly threw up, but, within minutes, the worst pain had eased and I was able to crawl back to the sofa, sit half up. He stared at me in wonder, asked,

"Where did you learn that?"

"On the beat on a Saturday night in Williamsburg."

He moved back, intimidated, asked,

"You were a cop?"

I nodded, sending pain right up to my brain. He said,

"I heard you were a priest."

"That too."

I had to know, asked,

"How come you were in an alleyway, brandishing a hurley? I am not complaining. Those fuckers were going to kill me and I heard one of them mention Keegan, whoever the fuck he is."

The skinhead, when you saw him properly, and when the brandy was coursing its magic in your blood, you realized how short he was, like five-two.

That is a fine height for a woman but a man, not so much.

He had a lot of ink, tattoos, and with the

Docs, red laces,

The ink,

His shaved head,

The suspenders holding up his too-short jeans,

He was like a gnome or a leprechaun gone Rambo.

He said,

"When your brother was shot, the killer shot a young boy too."

He wiped his nose of sniffles, his eyes welling up. I waited, then,

"That wee lad was my kid brother."

Blame the brandy, the crowbar in my face, but him calling anyone *wee* seemed absurd but, thank Christ, my face didn't display that thought.

I said, very quietly,

"I'm deeply sorry."

He acknowledged that by taking the brandy bottle and chugging it by the neck, got it down, burped, gasped,

"That's mighty."

"Why we drink it,"

I said.

He explained he was following me to see if the guy who shot my brother might have a go at me.

I guessed I owed him my life.

He said,

"You owe me your life."

As if he took the thought right out of mind. I asked,

"Who are you?"

He gave a bitter laugh, said,

"I'm a small man with a big hurley."

Indeed.

I gingerly touched my nose. It roared with pain, but it was reset.

God forbid, I am not gorgeous.

I asked,

"You know anything about baseball?"

He considered this, said,

"I love the Yankees."

Surprise and dismay seemed to halo this kid. I said,

"Shouldn't you be carrying a Louisville Slugger rather than a hurley?"

He gave a big smile and it transformed him from a somewhat surly, small man to a person of genuine warmth. There wasn't nastiness in him, a rare to rarest bonus.

He asked,

"What do I call you?"

"Mitch,"

I said.

"Most call me Mitch."

"Cool name, like you just have the one handle, like Madonna, Prince."

I almost said (blame the baseball reference), I almost said,

Call you shortstop?
Instead, I asked,
"What's your handle, pilgrim?"
He looked down at his Docs, long pause, then,
"Leeds."
I thought I misheard, which, when you've been battered by a crowbar and brandy, is not surprising. I thought he said,
"Leads."
As in *horse to water,*
Or,
Leads the field,
Or,
The UK word for a leash.
But no, he explained with a hint of shame, said,
"My dad was a Leeds supporter."
OK.
I said,
"That kind of means jack shit to me."
He smiled, said,
"I love how you Yanks talk."
"Really?"
He gave a huge grin, said,
"Oh yeah, like,
"Muthah-fuckah!
"And you gave us all the coolest stuff, like
"Zippos,
"Johnny Cash,
"Elvis,
"Coca-Cola,
"Milkshakes,
"ZZ Top!"
Fuck, we got the blame for ZZ Top?

He continued,

"Leeds were once the best, and I mean the absolute biz, the finest football team to come out of England and, under Don Revie, they were seriously legend. Alas, with a new manager, Brian Clough, not so shiny. They made a movie with Clough played by Michael Sheen."

This was a whole lot more info than I wanted or ever might get to use, so I lamely said,

"*Leeds*, hey, that's not such a bad name; got a ring to it."

He grimaced.

"Not if you grow up in Millwall."

I actually knew that name, because their supporters were infamous for their violence, giving a whole new glow to the term *hooligan.*

I was still feeling the effects of the crowbar to my head, said,

"I'm gonna brew some joe. Want some?"

He beamed, said,

"There you go. American language. I love it!"

I had the coffee simmering and Leeds was scanning my bookshelf, my meager one. He said,

"You have three books?"

They were:

Gerard Manley Hopkins,

Paulo Coelho,

Love in the Time of Cholera,

Oh, and a King James Bible.

Go figure.

He asked,

"Who is the Hopkins dude?"

How I'd have loved to see the faces of the literati if they heard Hopkins called *dude.*

I only ever had one item of value, not in the financial sense but in the form of an object that made me feel . . .

Pause.

Valued?

My first parish was in Williamsburg, a dangerous gig as the area was lethal then. My superior, name of Father Murphy helped me in so many ways. He liked to play up the image of the lovable, roguish Irish priest.

He was born in the Bronx; he was always astonished that a cop became a priest.

Not as amazed as my mother, but in there.

He liked to say,

"You're on the ecclesiastical beat now, Mitch."

Anyhow, on the eve of my departure from the parish, he came to my room, holding a leather book, worn, and well thumbed.

I said, bitterly,

"I'm all shot of Bibles, Father."

He laughed, said,

"Aren't you the bitter pill, lad."

Lad?

Part of his blarney schtick.

He said,

"I was going to give you *The Hound of Heaven*, but I think you already fled that beast so here is my own version of despair."

It was

The Wreck of the Deutschland

By

Gerard Manley Hopkins.

I read/studied it so many times, the leather was as worn as long-forgotten prayer.

I looked at Leeds, said,

"You can borrow it if you like."

And I was just about to launch into a long spiel on the poem, the poet, my interpretation, when he said,

"Naw."

Even now, all these deaths later, that moment still rankles. I wanted to shout,

You fucking ignorant punk!

But didn't.

I asked,

"Who are you, a skinhead who saved my ass, but what's your history?"

He drank some coffee, made slurping noises like they do in movies to demonstrate a villain, said,

"My old man was a Protestant, married a Catholic girl from Galway, and bingo, here I am."

I waited.

He said,

"They were not good parents: booze and beatings."

He looked at his hands, almost surprised to see,

    Love

      Hate

On his knuckles.

He continued,

"I was into hate, big-time hatred, joined a group who screamed White Supremacy, and they took me in, like fucked-up family, but I knew that gig."

He took out a pack of Old Virginia tobacco, some papers, looked at me, asked,

"Mind if I roll one?"

I said,

"Roll two."

He did so with a speed, ease, and expertise you could only have learned in prison.

He produced a silver Zippo, fired us up.

Nirvana.

I asked,

"What/who are you now?"

He gave a reluctant smile, said,

"I'm going to be your wingman for when we go hunting."

I nearly laughed, asked,

"Who are we hunting?"

He said,

"Keegan."

NO NATION IS

MORE POETICAL

OR

MORE RICHLY ENDOWED WITH FANCY.

—HERMANN VON PÜCKLER-MUSKAJU,
TOURING IRELAND, ENGLAND AND SCOTLAND IN
THE YEARS 1826, 1827, 1828, 1829

Kate had two opportunities to steal the gold cell phone from Dio.

The coveted cell that the combined forces of DEA, CAB, and Mason wanted.

And she didn't.

Why?

Truth to tell, she was relishing the rush of being with him. He treated her like royalty, forever flattering her, giving her a platinum credit card to

"do with as you wish."

Phew-oh.

Who in their right mind wouldn't want *just a teeny bit of time* with that?

And,

Whisper it,

She was developing a kind of crush.

No one, especially not Kate, saw that mooning down the drug-addled pike.

He made her laugh, and that was a rare to rarest commodity in Kate's life.

Mason.

Mason was mightily pissed, went,

"The fuck you playing at?"

They were in her cottage, decorated with brand-new clean, white furniture, megascreen TV, and flowers—flowers everywhere, delivered daily from Dio.

Kate said,

"You wanted me to go deep, get his trust?"

Mason was bitingly bitter, said,

"Did I include fucking him? Was that in your memo?"

Kate, never one to spin from a fight, lashed out, stung his left cheek hard.

Mason caught her wrist, said,

"One flick, your goddamn wrist is broken."

Truth was,

Yes,

She had slept with him.

Twice.

The first time, she put it down to drink.

OK.

The second, hmm.

Dio had a yacht, the most beautiful thing Kate had ever seen. It was sleek, painted blue and white, could sleep ten people and a crew of six.

Six!

They'd spent an afternoon on the bay. She got some rays, which would tan lightly, and in the evening, a candle-lit dinner on the deck, Galway bright and lovely on the horizon.

So, sleep with him, hell yeah.

Thing is, was she falling a bit in love?

Well, lust, for now.

Weird as it was, she felt validated. When you've been a junkie, validation is not coming down the pike very often.

And.

And this is the big and: *he made her laugh.*

Been a long time since that had happened.

Mason jolted her back to reality, said,

"You screw this up, don't get that golden phone, you're going to do at least ten in federal prison."

And time to wake her the fuck up, Mason said,

"We're fairly sure he had your aunt killed, had your brother shot, and we're hearing an attack was launched on your other brother, the ex-priest dude."

Kate just did not believe it, said to Mason,

"Why? I get why you want him, but why would he harm my family?"

Mason longed to shake her, rock the dumb out of her, said,

"Two reasons. One: he wants all obstacles removed, and two: he likes it."

He prepared to leave, said,

"Get your act together, nail him, and I don't mean in the bed."

He was gone.

Later in the day, Colin arrived. He was using a crutch, apologized.

"Sorry, sis, my leg went soft during my time in the hospital."

She lied, said,

"Hey, it suits you, gives you an air of mystery."

She managed to give him an awkward hug and felt like weeping.

She asked,

"Are you on painkillers?"

He nodded with a huge smile. She asked,

"The kind they urge you not to drink with?"

He said,

"Indeed, the best kind."

So, she broke the seal on a fresh bottle of Jameson.

With more than a sense of anxiety, Kate told Colin about her relationship with Dio. Colin's opinion on just about anything mattered to her. They had always been close, and when, as teenagers, their younger brother with Down syndrome died, they were the comfort of each other.

Neither of them was ever close to Mitch, he of a scholastic bend, whereas they lived for mischief and, basically, mayhem.

A tiny nudge of respect for him when he became a cop.

Tiny.

Colin, already a marine, did mock,

"You want to be a man, come deploy with me."

And then

Mitch left the cops and

Became

A priest.

The shame of it.

Colin's only words to Mitch were,

"What the fuck were you thinking?"

And Kate said,

"Don't become a kiddie-fiddler."

Then quit that profession!

Colin said,

"Nobody likes a quitter, but you, *you*, are setting a new world record for dropping out."

Mitch tried to explain, said,

"I lost my vocation."

Kate, disgusted, said,

"You lost your balls."

They were on their second drink when the doorbell rang. They looked at each other and, almost simultaneously, shrugged. The other side of two drinks, how worried can you be?

Kate opened the door to Mitch, stared at him for a moment, then,

"What do you want?"

Colin coming up behind her, said,

"Let the sad fucker in."

She did.

Mitch glanced at the bottle on the table, the glasses, asked,

"Celebrating?"

Colin sat, grabbed another glass, poured, said,

"Join in."

He did.

Knowing that to refuse would only fire up the air of resent-
ment already simmering. Kate raised her glass, said,

"Here's to the fucked-up family."

Colin asked,

"Why are you here, Mitch?"

He had a whole slew of answers, but none bordering on
civil, so he went with,

"I heard about our aunt's death, then a boyfriend of Kate's
being murdered, so I thought . . ."

He trailed off, not sure how to finish.

Kate said,

"And you're going to do what? Pray? Oh no, you got fired
from that gig."

Colin poured another round, said,

"The family that drinks together."

Mitch said,

"I got attacked a few days ago."

Colin asked,

"What happened?"

He told them and the guy mentioning the name Keegan.
Kate sat up, echoed,

"Keegan?"

Mitch nodded. She described Keegan, and Colin exclaimed,

"That's the guy who shot me!"

They both looked to Kate, who knew Keegan. She was quiet, then,

"Dio, the guy I . . ."

Pause.

"Am going out with . . ."

Pause.

"Sometimes,

"He has a second in command named Keegan."

Colin poured them another drink, said,

"Well, nothing complicated there. Kate's date is trying to kill her family. Why? Fuck knows?"

A knock at the door. Kate muttered,

"Who the fuck now?"

Opened it to a skinhead with a hurley. Kate said,

"We gave at the office unless the Mormons have had a whole overhaul."

Mitch said,

"That's Leeds. He saved me when I was attacked."

Colin asked,

"You're hanging with the Aryan Brotherhood?"

Leeds looked to Mitch, said,

"I've been tracking you, keeping an eye, but I got worried when you were in here so long."

Kate loved it, said,

"The priest and the skinhead. How very Claire DeWitt."

Colin said,

"Come in, son. You must be thirsty with all the protection gig."

Colin poured him a shot of the ever-dwindling bottle, said,

"To weird times."

All four eyed each other until Colin said,

"Let me describe the guy who shot me."

He did and saw Kate do a sharp intake of breath. She said,

"Oh my God, that's Keegan."

"Seems Kate's beau wants not to meet the family but to kill them."

Mitch was seated in a hard kitchen chair, next to Colin. Leeds was bouncing on his feet near the front door, fight or flight written on his face. Kate was in the middle of the room, between rage and confusion.

A voice behind them intoned,

"Well, this is one hell of a clusterfuck."

Mason, the marshal.

All heads turned to him. He said,

"I let myself in, and no need for introductions. I think I got that down."

Colin was on his feet, asked Kate,

"You know this joker?"

Kate explained, her voice sounding broken. There was a moment of stillness as each tried to digest the info and decide what next.

Leeds broke the spell, asked,

"No shit? You're, like, the real deal, packing heat?"

His attempt at an American accent amused Mason, who said,

"You're, what? A mini white supremacist? Don't you guys have a height requirement?"

Kate poured herself a drink, turned to face Mason, asked,

"So, what happens to Keegan? He's tried to kill my brothers."

Mason said,

"He's useful now, but you guys can have at him when we're done."

KEEGAN'S

RUN

Keegan stared at his two lieutenants who had failed to kill Mitch. They were nervous and looked like someone had kicked the shit out of them.

Named Troy and Danny, they had in the past been ferociously effective. Now they shuffled, made excuses. Keegan snarled,

"Tell me again what happened."

Troy, who was nursing a broken nose, said,

"It was all set to go down, then this guy appeared out of nowhere, knocked us sideways with a baseball bat."

Danny, the more nervous of the two, 'fessed,

"Troy let your name slip. He said *Keegan wants us to cut his throat.*"

Troy rounded on him, asked,

"What did you sell me out for?"

Danny shrugged.

Keegan had been perched on a wooden table. Now he reached back, produced a Glock, said,

"We have a dilemma."

Both men stared at the gun but said nothing.

Keegan said,

"A fuck-up like this, someone has to pay. A head has to roll and, I mean, how do we decide?"

The men looked at each other and not, it has to be said, with affection.

Danny said,

"I've been with you longer, boss."

Keegan reached back again and this time produced a machete, held the blade up to the light, said,

"I always thought this was an evil looking fucker, yeah?"

No word from the guys.

Keegan reached in his pocket, produced a euro coin, said,

"Call it and whoever wins gets to off the other, else I shoot the two of you."

The men eyed each other, then Danny rushed,

"Heads."

Keegan flipped it high and fast; it seemed to hold above them, then landed at Troy's feet.

Tails.

Keegan stood back, dropped the machete at Troy's feet, held the Glock on them both, said,

"The blade's been sharpened, so two full swings should sever the head."

He glanced at his watch, pushed,

"Let's go guys. Time is marching on."

Troy looked down at the blade as if mesmerized, but Danny grabbed it, sunk it in Troy's face, once, twice, then a third time.

Keegan said,

"Sly but impressive. Congrats. You lost but you win."

He turned as if to go, then said,

"I always liked Troy. You, not so much."

And

Shot him twice in the face.

Keegan knew time was seriously running out. Dio was like a maniac, seeing betrayal everywhere. When he heard Mitch was still alive, another botched attempt, he went on a rampage, destroying all around him.

And then . . .

Then he turned on Keegan, asked,

"When did you *actually* do something? I mean, besides fuck up everything?

Then Dio's face took on a more intense look and he moved toward Keegan. Keegan had his Bowie knife in his boot and began to edge his right hand toward it.

But Dio lunged, tore Keegan's T-shirt from his body, looking for a wire.

It was Keegan's favorite Guns N' Roses one.

Had been signed by Axl Rose.

Dio, as he stared at Keegan's bare chest began to rein in, tried,

"Dude, amigo, *hermano*, I'm out of line. I just lost it."

Keegan considered plunging the knife into the bottom of Dio's stomach, then ripping up to his chin and muttering,

Who's sorry now?

Dio hated to admit it, but his grand plan of meth conquest was in the toilet.

He had been freaked out when one of the users of his product managed to approach him with the meth mouth, teeth ravaged, the look of total madness on the face. Not that he gave a fiddler's fuck about their well-being; he just disliked having to *see* it.

He had told Keegan to start to wrap it up. Keegan asked, "What about the broad? The wannabe Callas."

Dio smacked him.

In the mouth.

A highly fraught moment hovered.

Dio and Keegan inhabited a supercharged world of violence and had

Seen

Witnessed

Initiated

All manner of mayhem.

But to each other?

Never.

A line was now crossed that set a whole new tone to their dealings. For the first time ever, Keegan felt like *the hired help*.

And Dio?

He felt he'd maybe, just *maybe*, made a catastrophic mistake.

He had.

Keegan was honing his knife.

The Bowie.

Long

Sharp

Serrated

Lethal.

Back in the day when Dio and Keegan were running coke out through Tijuana, they tried a risky one-off fast-and-dirty grab, trying to fly under the radar of the Gentlemen of Cali.

The deal was going down in a shed on the outskirts of the city when Keegan noticed one of the customers flick his fingers to his phone.

A tip-off.

Translated as,

There are only two gringos, come and waste them.

He said to Dio,

"*Hasta la vista.*"

Their code for

Incoming.

Shit going down.

But totally nuclear."

There were five Mexicans, and just Dio and Keegan. There were few things to get Dio *hotter* than being outnumbered.

These confrontations, rare though they were, got him *hot*.

He had once told Keegan he saw such confrontations like a chess board, and he and Keegan had the precision down to a fine art.

Keegan moved right into the Mexicans, the last thing they anticipated.

They were two gringos versus five of the most feared cartel. People did not run *at* them; they ran *from* them.

In a matter of seconds, Keegan had gut shot three of the Mexicans and Dio had shot the fourth in the face.

The fifth he knocked down, had his foot on the guy's chest, displaying his hand-tooled boots, and produced a rosary, dangled it over the Mexican's face, said,

"Pray, muthah fuckah."

Among the Mexican's mangled pleas could be heard,

"*Madre mia, Christos, del Corazón*," and, in truth, Christos featured most with *por favor* threaded in the whole pitiful imploring.

Keegan smiled. Begging turned Dio on.

He reached in his pocket, produced a thin cigarillo, lit it with the Zippo he'd gotten from the Zetas in the real

Glory

Gore-ridden

Days.

He leaned into the Mexican's face, asked,

"Mind if I smoke?"

No objections from the Mex.

On the Mexican's belt hung a Bowie knife, encased in a leather sling. Dio pulled it free, dropped ash into the Mex's face, said,

"Now, that is a fucking *knife.*"

Without even looking he flicked it high and hard to Keegan, who caught it in one smooth move.

These two guys worked together like a slickly oiled machine, honed by years of snaking through the cartels. Dio said,

"Now, my friend, if you ever decide to stab me in the back, remember who gave you the knife."

That was all too deep for Keegan, who shrugged.

A knife is a knife and all that.

Dio dangled the rosary beads over the Mex, asked,

"You want this cross?"

Then almost languidly, he knelt on the man's stomach and drove the crucifix into the man's right eye.

It was messy, gory, and some kind of yellow fluid mixed with brain matter and blood forced Dio step back to protect his pants from stain. He asked Keegan,

"That remind you of eggs over easy?"

Dio and Keegan had been a duo for a long time and knew each other as well as two stone killers can.

Keegan did, however, wonder if Dio got *too* euphoric about it. To Keegan it was his job, more or less, but definitely more business than pleasure.

Dio seemed to be deep in the getting-his-rocks-off area.

They'd stopped at a diner in El Paso and Keegan settled for coffee, but Dio?

Dio asked the waitress,

"How about a *Mexican blend?*

Grits

Sausages

Tomatoes.

With lashings of Tabasco sauce and peppers."
Paused. Then added,
"And eggs, way over easy."
Keegan doubted he'd ever touch an egg again. Ever.

AND

GHOSTS

MUST

DO

AGAIN

WHAT

BRINGS

THEM

PAIN

—W. H. AUDEN, "THE QUESTION"

The family summit, with Mason and Leeds in attendance, had come to three decisions:

Kill Keegan.

Well, not really. It was what we wanted, but we settled for:

1. Find Keegan and where he lived.

2. Confront him

3. Kate would continue to lure Dio.

Pretty lame.

All of it.

Those who knew Colin—that is, Kate and me—knew he was not into any kind of diplomacy and the above shit-poor resolutions were like Muqaddams whispering on a Galway breeze.

Or,

As the Texans say,

"All hat and no cattle."

The following day, I came out of my new apartment to see the Porsche idling in gear, Nora B in the driver's seat.

She asked,

"You like adventure?"

What fool would say no?

I had barely got in when she took off like the proverbial bat. She gunned that car like lethal intent. I had to ask,

"Maybe slow it down a tad?"

Sounding like an English wanker.

She laughed, said,

"You need to lighten up, padre."

Padre!

Man, I hated that, said so.

She moved one hand from the wheel, said,

"I have a surprise for you."

I have never quite drawn a line between a shock and a surprise; they seemed to ride together.

She hit a dial and the Pogues filled the car. She said,

"Kind of old-school, just for you."

I asked,

"And you listen to. . . ?"

She gave a slight smile, said,

"I need Metallica to jump my system."

I said,

"I never got the lure of head-banging music."

She made a gesture, indicating,

I rest my case.

Said,

"See? Old-school."

She continued to drive like a contender for some lunatic-of-the-year award.

"My dad, who left me a shitload of money, God bless his tight heart, liked to listen to some dude named Rory Gallagher."

Heresy.

I said,

"After I left the priesthood, I listened to the Ramones. Might be a New York thing."

She asked,

"When you were in the priest house, did you guys chant or some gig like that?"

I laughed, said,

"No, chanting wasn't part of the vibe."

She threw me a look, so I knew a question was coming. She asked,

"Why did you quit? I mean it's *hot*, but isn't it, like, hard to get out?"

I said,

"I couldn't hack it anymore."

We were entering Cong, said so on a signpost. I asked,

"What's in Cong?"

She said,

"My brother is buried here."

We bypassed the tiny village of Cong to a castle a few miles farther on. She said,

"This is Ashford Castle."

We drove up a long, impressive drive, stopped at the front of the castle. A valet appeared, greeted,

"How yah, Nora?"

She tossed him the keys of the car, said,

"Mind with your life."

He gave a high laugh and when we got out, he hopped in the driver's seat, took a moment, then drove off at speed.

I asked,

"They know you here?"

She gave a tiny smile, said,

"They know me most places. I'm a very generous tipper."

She said,

"Let us take the tour."

I do not know much about castles, they were scarce in Brooklyn, but this, even to my untrained eye, was absolutely fabulous. We walked through archways, fantastic gardens, and then came to the stables.

She asked,

"Wanna ride?"

She laughed as she said it.

Ride in Ireland has but one meaning.

Sex.

I could play, said,

"Maybe later."

We moved on to what Nora described as her

Favorite part.

Falcons.

Nora said, as she hugged the man caring for the birds,

"This is Brad; he's our falconer."

Two falcons were on a perch, their heads hooded. They seemed to give off a controlled ferocity, still but vigilant. Brad said to me,

"Our Nora here, she's a natural falconer. You ever had any experience with them?"

No.

Nora put on a thick, heavy glove, took one of the falcons on her outstretched arm, said,

"Let's fly this beauty."

We went into a meadow, with woods close by. Nora took the hood off, the falcon stared at me, staying perfectly still.

Then Nora muttered something, raised her arm, and the falcon flew.

It climbed impossibly high, until it was little more than a speck. I asked,

"How do you know she'll come back?"

Nora showed me pieces of meat, laid them on her arm, said,

"She knows me."

She used her left hand to point, said,

"Watch, she'll make her body fold into itself, dive with fierce speed in a straight line."

Nora braced herself. I was shitting myself. The bird seemed to be coming at me, all fierce power, deadly focus, then it veered, landed on Nora's arm. I went,

"Fuck me."

Nora said,

"Maybe later."

We spent three hours with the falcon, and three mesmerizing hours it was. The utter stealth and perfect predation of the bird were awesome.

Then we went to the hotel proper. The receptionist asked,

"Usual room?"

I looked at Nora, asked with more than a little cynicism,

"Your usual?"

She took a key card from the receptionist, said to me,

"I come here to chill."

I wanted to snarl,

"And to fuck."

She read my mind, said,

"No, you're the first. This is my private space. I'm wavering even now as to whether I should bring you."

I asked the obvious.

"Why me?"

She was heading for the elevators, me trailing behind, said,

"You're

"An ex-priest.

"Ex-cop."

She paused.

Then,

"What's not to fuck?"

And fuck we did.

Turned out we were staying the night.

Go figure.

I had no idea of exactly what the endgame of all this was. It certainly wasn't just a few days in the country to relax. Especially as Nora B for all her banter seemed to be under enormous strain. You grow up in a dysfunctional family, you know stress like you know your prayers in Irish.

Ingrained.

She was able to provide me with a clean sweatshirt and jeans that nearly fit me.

Her brother's, I presumed, but I did not ask.

Next morning, we had the full Irish breakfast.

Bacon.

Fried eggs.

Mushrooms.

Black pudding.

Sausages

Toast.

The country air had given me an appetite, but Nora B just drank black coffee and gave me looks of . . .

What?

Assessment?

Disappointment?

Breakfast done, with the staff tending to Nora like she was family. Me they gave cold veiled attention.

Efficient but ice.

Nora asked,

"You want to go shooting?"

In truth, I wanted to go home, but my small apartment hardly qualified as that, so I said,

"Sure."

During my year on the streets as a cop, my partner and I

hit the shooting range nigh every weekend, with six-packs to jack up our adrenaline. My partner asked,

"How'd you get to be such a hell of a shot?"

I said, mostly truthfully,

"I pretend they're family."

The hotel had its secluded area for clay shooting. The armorer, a jolly man named Theo, provided us with shooting jackets, explained how the shoulder padding softened the recoil, handed me a heavy, long-barreled shotgun and a roll of cartridges, asked,

"Need help?"

I said,

"Loading guns is the one skill I have."

I loaded up, shouted,

"Pull."

Out of eight discs, I hit seven. Theo gave a low whistle, said,

"Way to go, boyo."

Then Nora took her turn and hit all eight.

I said,

"Remind me not to piss you off."

The gun Nora used was a Remington. The stock had a silver motif, looked like a bird, the falcon perhaps. It was a beautiful weapon if "guns" and "beautiful" can coexist in the same sentence, never mind in the same breath.

On the butt were the initials "N. B."

I said,

"That is one impressive weapon."

Theo smiled, said,

"Specially made for our Nora."

Noticed the *our*.

Had to wonder about a world that makes shotguns for girls, but I kept that thought to myself.

She handed the shotgun to Theo, said to me,

"You'll be fine as long as I'm unarmed."

Words to live by.

We thanked Theo and I slipped him forty euro. He protested,

"There's no need."

I said,

"It's not about need, it's about respect."

And it was, kind of.

Nora said,

"Here's the final part of the tour and then we can get drunk."

I liked the sound of that a bit too much. Since arriving in Ireland, it seemed everything was the spur:

"To grab a pint."

I was not complaining; stopped me from wallowing in the old familiar guilt.

We walked as far as an impressive oak tree, a single white cross beneath the massive branches. We stood before the cross and she said,

"My gorgeous brother lies here."

What to say?

I said,

"I'm sorry."

She looked at me, near snarled,

"What are you sorry for? You didn't know him."

Word.

I felt that I should offer something, so went the stale,

"May he rest in peace."

A pause.

Then she snapped,

"Pieces."

WTF?

I thought I misheard, said,

"What?"

"Pieces. Twenty-five of them, if the autopsy was correct."

Jesus wept.

I staggered with,

"What/how/why?"

She looked right in my face, her expression pure granite, said,

"I guess they didn't like him much."

Before I could push, she said,

"Drink time."

And strode toward the hotel.

The hotel bar was huge. You could have fitted an AA meeting there and still have room for the undecided.

The barman, like all the staff, seemed delighted to see Nora. Me, not so much. He asked,

"The usual, darlin'?"

She said,

"Two of them. My friend here used to be a cop, then he was a priest."

The barman gave me a look of derision, said,

"Whatever floats your boat."

He began to build frozen margaritas. Don't get me wrong. I like the drink, but before noon? She read my mind, said,

"Lighten up, padre."

I had been struggling with my feelings for her. She was

Gorgeous.

Funny.

Unpredictable.

But I was tiring of her continuous efforts to shock.

Right then and there, I did not like her.

The barman was named Brad, same as the falconer's—what the hell?—and had a supercilious air. He put Nora's drink with great care on the counter and mine he literally plonked down, so it spilled. He looked at me, said,

"Whoops."

I was about at my limit of shit-taking. I grabbed his wrist, said,

"Brad, I did the night shift in Williamsburg and they spat out the likes of you for recreation, so go build me a fresh drink, then fuck off."

Nora touched my arm, said,

"That is so *hot.*"

I moved away from the counter, said,

"You have both drinks; I think you need them."

And . . .

And I walked out.

Of the bar.

The castle.

An ice-cold rage caught in my chest.

On the main road, I stuck out my thumb and, lo and behold, the first vehicle stopped. It was a white van, the worse for wear, and even more of a shock was the driver.

"Leeds!"

CALLOUS IS SIMPLY CRUELTY WITHOUT PLANNING AFORETHOUGHT.

Leeds was wearing a Galway United shirt, combat pants, and Doc Martens.

Ready to rumble.

I asked,

"How in hell can you be here? Did you follow me?"

"Yes."

A driver passed us at speed and Leeds leaned on the horn, shouted,

"Fuckhead."

I said,

"You're stalking me?

He looked at me, gave a huge grin, said,

"I'm protecting you. You know, like the Chinese say, you save a life then you are responsible for it."

I shook my head. This country is insane. I said,

"Protect me from Nora?"

He grimaced, said,

"Oh, yeah."

I had to know, asked,

"Where did you sleep last night?"

He indicated the back of the van, said,

"Got all I need there, even a Bunsen burner, you want me to stop, make coffee?"

Christ.

I asked,

"Protecting me from Nora? I mean, seriously?"

He caught up with the car that had overtaken us, drove alongside, brandished a heavy tire iron, and the car dropped behind. I mean, a skinhead shows you a jackhammer, would you front him?

I asked again,

"Nora?"

He gave a bitter laugh.

"She comes from a shitpile of money. I mean, at her age, a Porsche?"

I said nothing, so Leeds continued,

"Her brother crossed some drug dealer and they cut him to ribbons; pieces of the poor bastard all over the ground."

I asked,

"Anyone arrested for it?"

He looked at me, said,

"Get real, priest."

A song came on the radio that riveted me, tore at my heart for reasons I never even spoke. I asked Leeds,

"Who is that?"

He said,

"Corina K, a local girl. The title is 'One Million Scars.'"

The song finished and I felt

Bereft?

We arrived back in Galway; I realized my old clothes were left in the castle.

Not the kind of sentence I ever imagined I would write.

Dio had one large flaw in his streamlined security.

A red Camaro, lovingly polished and restored. That baby had an engine like a diesel. Open that sucker up on the motorway and fuck 'em all.

It amused Keegan to see his feared boss rave on about what Keegan called

A muscle car.

But worryingly for his bodyguards, he drove at reckless speeds and lost them more times than was safe.

Friday, the last one in September, Dio was traveling at warp speed when he heard a clunk in the souped-up engine.

"Fuck,"

He said.

He got out and was tinkering under the hood when he felt a figure approach. He half turned when he was shot in the face with a double-barreled shotgun.

It took his face almost clean away.

The figure stood over him, then spat on the body.

A tour bus came 'round the corner at speed and the killer panicked, dropped the rifle, vanished into the trees. The driver of the coach pulled up behind Dio's car, got out, and walked up to the body, and, without warning, shouted,

"Oh, fuck me!"

Indeed.

The tourists were swarming, amazed they saw what they read as *a victim of the Irish conflict.* One said to the very pissed driver,

"I thought the *Troubles* were over."

The driver looked at him, snarled,

"In Ireland, our troubles are never over."

When the Guards came, they found a fallen shotgun, dropped in a panic by the gunman.

BEING CALLOUS

DOES NOT NECESSARILY ENTAIL

A FEELING FOR NOIR

BUT IT DOES ADD THAT FRISSON

ESSENTIAL FOR THE

SHOCK OF NOIR NARRATIVE.

Keegan took the news of Dio's murder with a flurry of activity. Cover-up, cover-up, destroy, shred all documents, and surround himself with protection lest the killings were just beginning; such was the nature of the drug trade.

The list of suspects/enemies for the killing were legion.

Keegan mostly needed to run.

He had always felt the Irish branch of their business would bring trouble, but this? This was the worst turn of events and exposed Keegan in a way he had never been.

As second in command, you tended to stay in the shadows, safer there.

Keegan was hiding out in the Ocean Apartments, one of Dio's favorite crash pads. Keegan was gathering up the cash hidden all over the rooms. He heard a banging on the door, reached for the Glock on the table, pushed it into the back of his jeans, opened the door.

Mason.

The U.S. Marshal.

He gave Keegan a wide grin, pushed his way into the apartment, produced a bottle of Jack, said,

"Be a good boy, get us some glasses and take the weapon from your lower back. We don't want any . . ."

Pause.

"*Accidents.*"

Keegan laid the Glock carefully on the table, got two heavy glass tumblers, placed them on the coffee table. Mason uncapped the Jack, poured two liberal measures, asked,

"To what do we toast?"

Keegan gave a bitter smile, said,

"Survival."

Mason enjoyed that, drained his glass in one hit, said,

"Ah, heaven."

Keegan did not touch his drink, said,

"What's the deal now? My boss is dead. You wanted to nail him and he is indeed nailed."

Mason kept a shit-eating grin in place, asked,

"Did you kill him?"

Keegan gave a harsh chuckle, said,

"If I did it, there'd be no body."

Mason mulled it over, asked,

"How'd you like to be the boss?"

Phew-oh.

Keegan said,

"I'd like to get out. This seems the appropriate time."

Mason, still with the grin, said,

"You'd be able to help us with some other players."

Keegan shook his head. Mason said,

"You have heavy-duty jail time hanging over you."

Keegan put out his hands, said,

"Cuff me. I'm done with all this shit."

Mason considered him for a moment, then,

"Are you forgetting the Mitchell brothers, who are coming for you?"

Keegan said,

"No. They are one more reason to get out."

Mason said, as he prepared to leave,

"I think we'll let you swing in the breeze, see who peeps out."

He looked at the remaining hooch in the Jack bottle, said,

"Have a party."

And then, as if a thought just occurred, asked,

"Your late boss, the very dead Dio, once the autopsy is finished, any notion of what you want to do with him? No family came forward."

Keegan gave him a look, then,

"I'll take care of him."

Mason waited, asked,

"Fly him back to Mexico?"

Keegan scoffed, said,

"I'll burn the fucker."

Mason was a little taken aback, tried,

"Need any assistance with that?"

Keegan smiled, no *heat* in it, asked,

"Got a match?"

. . . And

The

Fire

Next

Time

Desperado!
Translates as
Callous.
Merciless.
All of which described Manuel Rodriguez. Head honcho of the newest Sinaloa cartel and main supplier to the late Dio.

Manuel was nicknamed "El Grillo" after he tied a rival drug boss to the front of a '54 Chevrolet, then drove the car at fifty miles an hour into a wall.

He was an oddity for several reasons.

A Mexican albino.

Exceedingly rare.

He loved the songs about the drug trade, the *narcocorridos.* Real fame or infamy to these psychos was to be the subject of one of the ballads.

El Grillo was currently top of the Mexican charts.

Go figure.

But he had a secret love of Johnny Cash. Due perhaps to the only prison stint he had endured, and one of the incarcerated had a tinny radio that seemed stuck on Cash, no pun intended.

> *There's a man going 'round*
> *Taking names.*

El Grillo saw himself as that dude.

El hombre de negro.

The Man in Black.

He dressed in black, had his hair dyed jet-black, black shades, and was the spit of Roy Orbison.

To suggest this to him was to end up on the grille of another classic car.

In the barbarous stakes, it was hard to be the market leader. The photo that went viral of six bodies hanging from an overpass. It was even suggested they were a family, as if the horror level were not sufficient.

Top that!

El Grillo had a family hanged by their heels, not an easy task, and just before the bodies were slung over the bridge their throats were cut simultaneously and the torrent of blood flooded onto the passing cars like some malevolent Stephen King scenario. A family (another) had its windshield blinded, the father veered off the road, was hit by an oncoming truck, then a line of cars pulped into one another.

Total casualties: forty-six dead.

El Grillo was the man.

Keegan was mystified. He couldn't figure how Dio could have been so easily assassinated. Not just killed but *assassinated*.

Men like Dio couldn't merely be killed. Sure, his enemies were fucking downright legion, count 'em, including Keegan his own self.

But he needed Dio, not least because the freaking federal government would put his ass in jail if he didn't deliver Dio to them.

Plus, he might be next on the assassin's list.

He'd tripled his own security, but no fucking good if they couldn't protect Dio.

He poured himself a stiff tumbler of tequila from a

bottle supposed to be fifty years old. Dio would occasionally take a sip from it and extol its virtue for at least a woeful half hour.

He'd say,

"Paisan, this is the very liquid from the ground of Sinaloa."

It had been given to Dio by Joaquin Guzmán, a direct honor, but little use to El Chapo now, languishing in a supermax.

The cartels lived and died with terror as their modus operandi. But one thing truly scared them shitless.

Supermax.

If Keegan had to face that, he'd off himself first.

Keegan had *grilled* the bodyguards assigned to Dio. They hailed from Germany, and you'd expect German efficiency, but they had been diverted by a motorcycle strewn on the road between their car and Dio's.

Dio refused to be driven, quipped,

"I'm driven enough."

You laughed, of course. *El patron* tried humour, you laughed like a hyena.

But no jokes, bad or otherwise. No more.

He warned the Germans,

"El Grillo is arriving this week. Have a brilliant defense ready."

The Germans were not impressed. They were graduates of the Stasi and didn't frighten easily; they were the ones who gave the frights.

So they believed.

A mansion had been secured behind the golf course for El Grillo. He had specified he wanted a large garden, said,

"Get me a spit that cooks pigs."

* * *

Late in November, residents of homes close to the manor inhabited by El Grillo found their senses near assailed by a horrendous stench, like some animal was on fire.

They were partially right.

Three Germans were on a large spit, turning slowly, watched by Keegan and a crew of Dio's most trusted.

In drug circles, *trust* was a hugely loose term.

In one of those quirks of nature that seems to approve of evil, a strong wind had come across Galway Bay, dissipating the noxious fumes, partly if not completely.

One of the crew had asked, eyeing El Grillo with extreme caution,

"Is that Roy Orbison?"

Keegan indicated the spit, said,

"You want to join them, ask El Jefe that."

He didn't ask.

When the event, if such a term can be applied to this, wound down, El Grillo pulled Keegan aside, asked,

"Who were the citizens involved in your feeble attempts to dispose of them?"

Keegan knew this was what is termed

A loaded question.

Keegan hadn't survived the Zetas, Dio, and numerous psychos of every hue to let such a question throw him. He gave a brief summary of the two Mitchell brothers, of Kate, and the preceding dance between all of them.

El Grillo took off his shades, revealing eyes that seemed to look inward and had a glint that made your very soul shake. El Grillo was aware of this effect, took a moment longer of locking eyes with Keegan, said,

"I'm not a fair man, but you may have surmised this."

His accent sounded like he had learned his English from

Masterpiece Theatre and had a dramatic pause before he continued, said,

"Bring me all their heads. You have a week."

Keegan was put in mind of an old movie he'd caught on cable:

Bring Me the Head of Alfredo Garcia.

Dark, violent, and utterly nihilistic.

Keegan loved it, in part because the actor Warren Oates reminded him of his old man. A biker, robber; he never met a crime he didn't take a shot at. Between jail stretches, Keegan had caught up with him in El Paso and they went on a tequila binge.

He changed names as often as he changed cars, so . . . a lot. Currently, or back then, he was trading under the name Joel.

There was some question as to whether he was Keegan's father, but they both were happy to assume it so.

He'd shacked up with Keegan's mom. Along came Keegan, so Joel took responsibility. Keegan's mom was, as they say, *active.*

Joel did not fixate on her promiscuity, as she had the quality he most admired in a woman:

Humor.

Keegan did not admire many—in fact, nobody—but he had a great liking for his old man, who taught him to drive, fish, play ball, and how to clean and reload a pistol in just under two minutes.

A true life skill.

And

He made

Keegan

Laugh.

A lot.

It was Joel who'd advised him,

"Do not fuck with the cartels."

Keegan was mid-crawl up the Zeta ladder at the time.

Keegan and his old man did a blitz of bars along the Rio Grande, Joel driving a '96 Buick that he tooled to resemble a muscle car, the engine souped up to a perilous degree.

If happiness was a feeling Keegan rarely had trade with, then that day—though both men would have scoffed at the term—a *bond* was forged.

Alas and alack, as they mutter in Galway, it was to be the last time.

Joel pulled a jolt in Attica and got on the wrong side of the Aryan Brotherhood (is there a *right* side?) and was shivved to death in the yard.

With a blade burned into a toothbrush.

With no one to claim the body—Keegan was deep in the Zetas then—Joel was buried in the prison yard, something very poignant in the fact he'd never, even in death, leave the prison.

His beloved Buick was stolen by a Black pimp, who totaled it on an L.A. freeway.

An American short story all in itself.

EVERYTHING IN NATURE

IS LYRICAL

IN ITS IDEAL ESSENCE.

TRAGIC IN ITS FATE

AND COMIC IN ITS EXISTENCE.

—GEORGE SANTAYANA, "CARNIVAL"

As kingfishers
    Catch fire.
    Gerard Manley Hopkins.

    I don't know why, but those lines always set me on fire, in a yearning, haunting, almost mystical fashion.

    I had the misfortune to once mention this to Colin. He answered,

    "Shite talk."

    But to be fair (whenever anyone says that you can bet fair is the very last thing they intend) he did find and give me the battered leather copy of

    The Wreck of the Deutschland.

As thus we were gathered to discuss Keegan, and what the fuck was to be done with him.

    Gathered in the house was as diverse a crew you could fathom.

    Kate.

    Nora B.

    Colin.

    M'self.

    Leeds.

    A brief appearance from Mason.

    And behind Colin were two hard-looking men, wearing U.S. fatigues with the insignias torn off, but I still make out sergeant major and, maybe, first lieutenant.

    Colin said,

"The sergeant is Costello from the old neighborhood, and the other is from my unit; they got called . . .

"Abbott and Costello."

Colin said,

"Costello is chatty when he's the other side of Jack (Daniel's, of course) but my good buddy here, the Taliban got him, and we were slow in rescuing him."

He paused, then,

"The dirty bastards cut his tongue out and, trust me, we made the Alijah Province burn for three fucking days."

Abbott smiled at the memory.

Colin, still weak from the two bullets he had taken, continued,

"These guys will take care of Keegan, and the marshal"— he indicated Mason—"will do what his macho buddies do."

To say the air was tense is putting it mildly.

Mason was standing, cowboy pose, fingers hooked into his belt, which featured a Texan buckle with steer horns. It was more Village People than macho.

He said,

"Here's the deal, people: nobody touches Keegan. Hands off. This is a federal case."

I laughed, said,

"You're in Ireland. They could give a fuck about your jurisdiction."

On that note, Mason took a deep breath, said,

"I'm not feeling the love here, guys, so I feel it incumbent to share at a deeper level to kick-start a sense of family and those of you not knowing what *incumbent* means, don't ask Colin's tongue-less buddy. We don't want to dwell on folks' shortcomings, but . . ."

Pause.

"But best to put it out there. Our winsome Kate over there, all hot and simmering, well, dear reader, I fucked her and *she*"—he mimed a drum roll—

"She fucked Dio every which way."

Abbott moved like a panther, dark and fast, had Mason on the ground, Mason's head in the lock. Abbott's other hand produced a long, jagged-edge knife and sliced deep and long into Mason's face, then let him go.

Everyone was full-on shocked, save for Colin and Costello. Colin said,

"As he can't speak, he needs to send messages in another fashion."

Costello and Colin moved fast to stanch the blood oozing from Mason. It was deep and lengthways down his right cheek.

I went to help, and Colin snarled,

"No civilians, back the fuck off."

After ten minutes, many bloodied towels, much grunting, they stood, said,

"That should do the trick."

I risked looking at Mason, who was unconscious, the deep gash along his face sealed.

"How?"

Costello smiled, said,

"Superglue."

Leeds said,

"Awesome."

Kate asked if Mason had passed out, and now Colin smiled, said,

"I punched his lights out. No one—no one—talks trash about my sister."

Leeds said,

"I wanna join your gang."

Colin and his crew emphasized they would deal with Keegan and his cohorts. I asked,

"What are Leeds and I to do?"

Colin looked to his buddies, some private joke going there, and I figured I was the butt of it. He said,

"You can pray for us, pretend you're still a priest."

The derision was palpable.

Leeds, well fed up with the commands and orders, snapped,

"We'll do what the fuck we think is right. You'd do well to stay out of our way."

There was silence for a moment, then the trio laughed. Costello moved up close to Leeds, said,

"Don't get in our way; we don't allow for civilians."

Colin, who seemed to have elected himself leader, said to Kate,

"You lie low. Dio is dead, and there are those who might feel you had some part in it."

Kate, rarely a follower, snapped,

"And you, you'll keep me safe? Keegan has already shot you twice."

Colin took it well, said,

"Abbott will stay with you until we end it."

Kate looked at the man whose tongue had been torn out, asked,

"And he is going to talk to me . . . how?"

His buddy Costello answered,

"Abbott didn't talk even before the mutilation. You won't even know he's around."

Unconvinced, she snarled,

"A man in my home, I notice."

I felt I should add to the discussion, asked,

"What about me and my wingman, Leeds?"

Colin, alongside his lethal buddies, sneered,

"You can pray for us, pretend Leeds is your altar boy."

Colin said,

"We have a house off Grattan Road, plenty of room if anybody needs to crash."

Then he and his buddies were gone.

Leeds looked at me, asked,

"We're not going to do what that shithead says, are we?"

I said,

"We'll stay out of their way, get all the info we can on Keegan."

Kate looked at Nora B, said,

"Notice how the guys make plans, just presume we'll be along for the ride."

Nora B smiled, said,

"It was always so; doesn't mean we have to do jack shit."

Kate said to me,

"You and your little leprechaun need to leave too."

I asked,

"No coffee?"

Nora and Kate volunteered to take Mason to the hospital. He was still in deep shock and went without a word.

The
First
Bank
Robbery

The First National Bank in Clifden held a ton of money on the second Thursday of every month. It handled salaries for the big companies that ringed the area. Security was two guards, formerly of army service.

Three tellers and the manager comprised the staff.

At 9:15 on Thursday two heavily armed men wearing balaclavas rushed into the bank, shooting into the air and screaming obscenities.

The staff were forced to lie on the floor with the two security guards.

Shock and awe were the modus operandi of the men, and it worked, perfectly.

Five minutes, tops, and they were out of there, into a green van, driven by a third figure.

By the time the Guards arrived, the gang was long gone, the van found burned on a side road.

Estimates of the haul ranged from a hundred thousand to half a million.

Serious cash.

A Garda superintendent hinted at paramilitary links.

He also said,

"We are following definite leads."

They weren't.

The papers focused on the efficiency of the raid and suggested a military-style operation.

I had only the vaguest knowledge of this as I read the papers in the pub. I was a regular there by now, I was still referred to as *the Yank*, but with no malice riding point.

Leeds arrived, excitement writ large, led the way to a snug for privacy, and near shouted,

"You know I've been following Colin and his thugs."

I did not.

I said,

"You've got to be crazy. Those guys are dangerous. Trust me, you do not want them to know you're in their business."

He was excited, dying to tell me his news, said,

"I saw them steal a green van and guess what? That van was used in the bank heist."

Colin and his buddies were robbing banks?

I said,

"Leeds. Leeds, listen to me: if those guys are robbing banks, you do not want to be a witness."

He was offended, hurt by my nonappreciation, said,

"What is your plan? Let them do what they like?"

Pretty much, in truth.

I tried,

"We have to locate Keegan, let the cops deal with him."

He was way down disappointed, accused,

"You're afraid of them. You used to be a cop. How can you be so . . ."

Pause.

He fumbled for the right word, settled on,

"Useless?"

I said, lamely,

"We'll think of something, something less risky."

He was disgusted, stormed out, muttering,

"Coward."

I went to Colin's new house, and new it was. As in, recently built.

Knocked on the door, opened by Abbott, who waved me into a large front room. And the first thing I saw was stacks of money lining one wall. Colin appeared, shadowed by Costello. He indicated the money, asked,

"Need a loan?"

On the floor were what appeared to be a stockpile of weapons.

Uzis.

AKs.

Handguns.

I asked,

"Expecting a war?"

Colin went to the coffee pot, poured some, said,

"Just the cartel."

I looked 'round, said,

"This is. Insane."

Costello said,

"We do crazy."

I said,

"Keegan has gone to ground; you're wasting your time."

Costello said,

"We'll keep busy knocking over banks."

Fuck.

Kate did not know how she felt about the death of Dio. She had to admit he'd been growing on her, and the edge he possessed was exciting. She was in her house, drinking coffee with Nora B. She said,

"I never thought I'd be sorry for him."

Nora scoffed, said,

"He was a drug-dealing psycho; no shortage of them."

Kate changed tack, asked,

"You're seeing my brother?"

Kept her tone mild, as if it were no big thing.

"Fucking,"

Said Nora.

"I was fucking him. No great love affair."

Kate was shocked that she was shocked. She had herself down as chill, but this, I mean, c'mon.

She tried,

"Whatever."

And Nora smiled.

SOME ARE BORN CALLOUS.

OTHERS, BY THE HORRORS THEY HAVE WIT-

NESSED.

BUT ONE THING IS FOR SURE:

IT IS NOT A TREATABLE CONDITION.

Colin and his crew were taken down.

I had dropped the dime.

When Colin and the boyos entered the Bank of Ireland in Clifden, the armed response unit was waiting. Both Abbott and Costello were wounded and, seeing that, Colin surrendered.

They were held in the new jail on the outskirts of town, top security.

I didn't visit.

Leeds was the only one who knew I was the informant. Or, as Leeds said,

"The rat."

He was pretty much disgusted with me, said,

"Your own brother."

I tried,

"I was trying to save his sorry ass."

Leeds scoffed,

"So, he'll get life in jail. I'd say he will be super grateful."

Lamely, I shot,

"Family, it's complicated."

Leeds was infuriated, spat,

"You think I'm some sort of orphan?"

Before I could answer, he shook his head, said bitterly,

"I was going to offer you a partnership in an agency, like you know, PIs."

The worst thing of all, I laughed. The idea was balls-to-the-wall insane. Leeds stared at me, then with a soft *fuck you,* he was gone.

Long after he'd gone, I found a crumpled card and when I flattened it out, I saw,

MITCHELL AND LEEDS
INVESTIGATIVE AGENCY

There were two cell-phone numbers.

Holding that battered card in my hand, my heart was shrived.

The oddest thing, I'd become a regular in Garavan's. Not exactly my own stool but in the neighborhood. I could even call the barman by name (Sean), and I remained *the Yank*.

Over a few weeks, a man named Fallon had become almost a friend. I say *almost* because in Ireland they always kept you just slightly off balance.

It was three weeks into our friendship before he told me he was a Guard, and not just your run-of-the-mill beat cop, but a detective.

For one crazy moment, I wondered if he was investigating me.

Paranoia gets bad press, but it does keep you sharp.

When he told me, I said,

"I was a cop."

He laughed, said,

"The whole town knows that."

Fuck.

He said,

"NYPD is highly respected in this city. You guys are heroes because of TV shows, 9/11, and myth-making."

I said, without rancor,

"I'm no hero."

He smiled, asked,

"Who the fuck is anymore?"

But I had a friend and the difference between one friend and none is infinity. I think I learned that shite at priest school. It was the sort of theological horse shite we passed off as discourse.

I bought the next round of drinks, asked him,

"You know a kid name of Leeds?"

He laughed and took a sip of the fresh pint of Guinness, said,

"Your skinhead sidekick."

Before I could confirm, he continued,

"Gay little fucker."

What?

He stared at me, said,

"Jeez, you didn't know? Christ almighty, how could you not know? You sure you were a cop?"

I showed him the crumpled card Leeds had given me, outlining a PI agency, and expected more sarcasm but he went another route, said,

"Not the worst idea. We had a PI here until the drink took him out, but he always had tons of work, so if you plan on sticking around, it could fly."

He echoed,

"Mitchell and Leeds. Has a ring to it, not to mention the notion of a Nazi skinhead and a failed priest being private dicks."

He let that double entendre simmer, then called the next round. His cell rang and he answered, glowered, agreed to something with gruff grace, ended the call with,

"I'm on my way."

I asked,

"Work?"

He weighed this, decided to let a little seepage flow, said,

"The killing of that head honcho, with a shotgun, there might be a break in the case."

I asked,

"A suspect?"

He looked at me, gauging my trustworthiness, gave,

"The butt of the shotgun, it had initials: an intricate carving of a falcon."

Oh fuck.

I said, without thinking,

"N.B."

He stopped in his tracks, asked,

"You know who it belongs to?"

I had to think fast, tried,

"Those cartel dudes, they sign their work, and that *NB* was about fourth in line in the vacant spot."

He didn't believe me but figured it was not the time to push, said,

"We'll speak deeper, buddy."

And was gone.

I was a drink past tipsy so left the pub myself.

Just around the corner from the pub was St. Nicholas Church, home to the Protestants, and, on a whim, I went in, lit some candles.

I lit them and couldn't find a slot for the payment, so unlike the Catholic gig of

Give

And often

And a lot.

There was a peace in the church, a church seven hundred years old, and I lingered in a pew for longer than I'd planned.

I nearly smiled, thought,

An ex-priest sitting in a Protestant church, lighting free candles.

It was almost a country song.

The rector, a young brunette, spoke to me, asking if I needed a blessing.

She was blessing enough her own self.

When I got back to my house, I was startled to see a young Labrador tied to my door. I muttered,

"The fuck is this?"

There was a note under the dog's collar. I bent down to retrieve it and the dog gave me a furtive lick that kind of melted my heart. The note said,

You need one friend; his name is on the medal on his collar.

I rubbed the dog behind his ear, read the medal, his name, one word,

Revie.

Who the fuck was Revie?

And, mainly, I would have to stop saying *fuck.*

THE BANSHEE IS MENTIONED BY THE LATE JOHN

O'DONOHUE

IN HIS SUPERB BOOK, *ANAM CARA*.

HE SPECULATES THAT

THE OLD CELTIC TRADITION

FUSES THE

PHYSICAL

AND

SPIRITUAL

WORLD TOGETHER.

What to do with Nora?

Shop her.

Good Lord, I'd just snitched my brother to the Guards. Was I now to sell her down the river? She blew Dio's head off and would probably get away with it if I said nothing.

I phoned her. She answered almost immediately. I asked, "Fancy a pint?"

She was Irish, she most always was up for that.

She suggested McSwiggan's in Woodquay.

The weather was getting very cold, so I wore the all-weather Garda coat, collar turned up, making me every inch the private investigator or the informant.

An Irish person would have been more succinct.

As in, *arsehole*.

I had a Galway United shirt, blue jeans that were turning white from time and faulty washing. I had recently bought a pair of Doc Martens. Docs were having a moment, with all the cool kids now purchasing them.

I had managed to get a vintage pair with—get this—

Steel toe caps rather than Steel magnolias.

As a new dog owner, I put down water and a bowl of his daily food. The past week, I had purchased

A leash.

Dog license.

Dog food.

After a hundred hours of walking him, I felt we were bonding. Soon, I would be able to take him for walks, maybe without the leash. I was more than a little delighted with him.

I had never owned a dog.

In Brooklyn, they ate them.

Our preferred romp was along the beach. You started at the end of Grattan Road, coursed along the sand of Salthill, and ended under the diving boards at Black Rock.

I'd look out across Galway Bay and yearn.

For what?

Love.

Success.

Who knew?

When you've been a cop and then a priest, you're kind of running out of options. I felt tremendous guilt about selling my brother down the river.

I was sitting on a rock near the water as the dog cautiously tested his paw in the water, looked back at me, like,

Whatcha think?

I said,

"Very cold this time of the year."

A man out jogging, stopped, wiped his brow, guzzled water, said,

"How yah?"

The warm Irish greeting, it was less a question but more a general catch-all greeting, and it was sexless, applied to all. I said,

"Doing good."

I wasn't.

Waited for the inevitable,

"You're a Yank?"

He offered me his thermos and I said,

"I'm fine, but thanks."

He said,

"It's not water."

He asked,

"Are you familiar with *uisce bheatha*?"

No.

I said,

"No."

He was still holding the flask out, said,

"Translates as 'holy water,' or you might be more familiar with poitín?"

I was, said,

"Irish moonshine."

He laughed, said,

"Aye, but I think you'll find this more lethal."

I took the flask and risked a sip. Fuck, paint off a gate. I coughed and he said,

"Get a good drop in yah; there's plenty."

I fake-drank some more, said,

"Thank you, Mr.. . . ?"

Revie had come back from the water's edge and was now rolling in a stray patch of grass amid the sand. If I had drunk the poitín, I might have rolled there my own self.

He said,

"I don't normally hand out my name to strangers, but we've split a drink so I think it's OK."

But he didn't.

Give me his name.

Asked,

"Nice dog, whatcha call him?"

I said,

"Revie."

He made a sign of the cross in mock dread, said,

"Don fucking Revie."

Everyone knew who this Revie guy was. I asked,

"I should know who that is?"

He was incredulous, said,

"Only the best manager English soccer ever had. The glory days of Leeds."

I whistled for the dog, put on his leash, said to the guy,

"Good chatting with you."

He waited until I was a few yards away, then,

"Check out the movie with Michael Sheen as Revie."

Yeah, sure.

I did know the actor from the movie

Frost vs Nixon.

But didn't say that, and the guy shouted after me,

"Why are you Yanks always so naïve?"

For a moment I considered going back and giving him a *puck in the mouth.*

In Ireland, a *puck* was a punch with serious intent.

But he did share his drink, so there was that. I let it slide.

The heavens opened and in minutes me and the dog were drenched. I said to Revie,

"'Tis soft Irish rain."

Truth to tell, my Irish accent was atrocious.

I was torn over what to do about Nora—the initials on the shotgun and the moral question

Should I rat her out?

I was more afraid of what the cartel would do than the cops. If, and a terrible if, she went to prison, the cartel could easily put a hit on her.

I got to my building and thought for a moment I was back in Brooklyn.

A Crown Vic parked there.

Unlike the battered models we used as cops, this one was in good condition. The dog looked at me, sensing my distress. I rubbed his ear and he was quiet.

The door of the car opened and for one ghastly, or rather ghostly, moment, I half expected my dead partner to step out.

Nora B.

She tossed me the keys, said,

"Happy birthday."

I said, lamely,

"It's not my birthday.

She laughed, said,

"If I got a free car, I'd believe it was my birthday."

True.

Then she bent down, took the dog's face in both hands and muttered several soft sounds. The pup was instantly smitten.

I knew the signs.

In my apartment, I asked,

"Seriously, you're giving me a car?"

Who does that? hung on the back of my question.

She said,

"Are we not an item, a couple, betrothed or . . ."

Pause.

"Just fuck buddies?"

I thought,

The mouth on her.

The thought was in Brooklynese. How'd that happen?

Oh, yeah, the Crown Vic.

She sat on the sofa in that fashion some women do, with their legs tucked under them like DIY yoga.

I asked,

"A drink?"

She said,

"A big one."

I offered her ice with her Jameson. I didn't have any but felt it was polite to offer. She curled up in a ball of mock horror, fake screamed,

"Ice in Jameson? The heresy of it!"

I poured large amounts, handed her a glass. She took a healthy swig of it, sighed, said,

"Better."

I asked,

"Why on earth would you give me a car?"

She seemed confused, as if the question were insane, said,

"You spoke of Crown Vics being the cop car you preferred, so I was shopping for cars and voilà, Crown Vic."

I echoed,

"'Shopping for cars?' Sounds like a Snow Patrol song."

She held out her glass for a refill. The girl could drink, and I wasn't far behind, as the murder of Dio was there in the room, waiting for me to say it.

But I played for time, tried,

"I can't accept it."

She truly was mystified, said,

"I've shitloads of money, you have nothing, so it balances out."

OK. I bristled at her saying I had *nothing*, reined in my anger, said,

"I've a dog."

And she laughed, said,

"And just the cutest thing. The dog is nice, too."

Maybe the booze hit me too fast, or it was nerves, but I just blurted,

"I know you killed Dio."

The words hung there, like minute particles of ice. Nora sat up straight, looked like she was going to deny it, swerved, asked,

"How do you know that?"

I said with a heavy heart,

"Your initials on the shotgun."

She laughed, said,

"Oh, silly me."

Then a thought hit her and she near wailed,

"You are going to turn me in?"

I was considering it, and feeling awful about even harboring the idea. I said,

"You blew his head off. I mean, it's serious shit."

She stared at her feet. I pushed,

"Why the hell would you risk everything to kill a drug dealer?"

Her head still down, she said,

"He was my father."

Now that's a showstopper. I echoed,

"Your father?"

She held out her glass with shaking hands. I poured her third drink, but who was counting?

She gulped, said,

"Years ago, he was actually married but if you deal with the cartel, a family puts you on the firing line so he walked away and for years he sent mountains of money to keep us quiet but primarily to keep us unknown. My brother . . ."

She paused.

"My gorgeous brother, Johnny, a gentle soul, died from bad heroin supplied by my dear daddy's crew."

She was gasping for air, tears rolling down her cheeks, making a soft plink against her glass, like the music of utter despair.

I said quickly,

"I won't rat you out."

She was silent, then composed herself, drew herself up, asked,

"And what, I'm supposed to be grateful?"

Then added,

"I had a plan for us today: drive down to the Cliffs of Moher, and I got an old-style picnic basket, filled it with goodies. But now. . . ?"

She stood up, said,

"I have to go."

There are a hundred things I could/should have said, but I didn't.

She picked up the keys to the Crown Vic, said,

"Guess you won't accept a gift from a killer."

And was gone.

It would be two days before I heard of a young woman driving over the Cliffs of Moher. It was believed she crashed through a barrier, looking for a picnic site.

Anyone with information on a Crown Vic was asked to get in touch with the Guards.

I sat in a chair and literally howled like a broken banshee.

THE SIGN ON THE DOOR

SAYS

COME AS YOU ARE,

BUT

I DOUBT IT.

—MATTHEW WEST, *TRUTH BE TOLD*

Kate was in hell. No matter where she turned, there was death and injury.

Nora B, dead.

Dio, dead.

Her brother shot and now in jail.

Her older brother had been attacked.

Her fictional heroine, Claire DeWitt, was no help now. Kate felt Claire had abandoned her in Brooklyn.

This *new life* in Ireland was seriously fucked.

Her doorbell went and she wondered what fresh disaster was waiting.

Her brother, Mitch; disaster enough.

She led him in, offered a drink, settled for coffee.

"So?"

She asked,

"Who did you sell down the river now?"

He tried to broach the subject of Nora, said,

"I'd no inkling she'd kill herself."

Kate gave a bitter chuckle, said,

"You sold your own brother, why would a girl who simply liked you be any different."

He tried,

"Kate, there's just us two now. We should stick together."

Kate said,

"I didn't like you when you were a cop, even less when you were a priest, and now as a snitch, well, you figure out how that plays."

He made the awful mistake of moving to hug her and she reacted forcefully, said,

"Are you mad? A hug?"

Kate looked at him with utter contempt. He let his arms slump down, said,

"You know where I live if you change your mind. I'm always here for you."

She made a face, went,

"When, like, one time, were you *there for me*?"

He couldn't, turned to go. Kate said,

"Colin is hoping to get released."

He was stunned, said,

"When, how?"

She gave a bitter laugh, said,

"The arrest warrant was screwed up."

He asked,

"And his buddies?"

"Not so good for them."

Mason, the U.S. Marshal whose face had been slashed by one of Colin's buddies, developed a fearsome infection and was in such bad condition that they shipped him home.

With Dio dead,

Mason out of his life,

Things might have seemed to be better for Keegan.

Nope.

The new top dog, El Grillo, was beginning to look at him with those hooded eyes that spelled nothing good. Keegan, without a word to anyone, took the boat to England, stayed in one of those transit hotels in London, arranged a flight to Switzerland, and went there to visit his money.

He'd dumped all his phones but was tempted to keep Dio's, the one that held so much data, but figured cell towers might lead pursuers to him, so he binned it in Brixton.

Keegan had completed his business in his Zurich bank, came out, and started to cross the street when he was hit by a car. He didn't die instantly but had enough time to register the make of the car, muttered with his dying breath,

"Daimler. A fine model."

I was at home, sipping on a brew, trying to figure out the next step in my life, rummaging in my jacket, I found the crumpled card

MITCHELL AND LEEDS

INVESTIGATIVE AGENCY

I thought about it, then picked up my phone, dialed the number, heard Leeds's voice. I took a deep breath, asked,

"You still up for the investigation gig?"

My father had always said,

"Be able to call yourself something." And I had tried

Cop.

Priest.

Brother.

Just maybe a crazy idea would be the way to go.

ABOUT THE AUTHOR

Ken Bruen (b. 1951) is one of the most prominent Irish crime writers of the last two decades. Born in Galway, he spent twenty-five years traveling the world before he began writing in the mid 1990s. As an English teacher, Bruen worked in South Africa, Japan, and South America, where he once spent a short time in a Brazilian jail. He has two long-running series: one starring a disgraced former policeman named Jack Taylor, the other a London police detective named Inspector Brant. Praised for their sharp insight into the darker side of today's prosperous Ireland, Bruen's novels are marked by grim atmosphere and clipped prose. Among the best known are his White Trilogy (1998–2000) and *The Guards* (2001), the Shamus award-winning first novel in the Jack Taylor series. Bruen continues to live and work in Galway.

KEN BRUEN

FROM MYSTERIOUSPRESS.COM
AND OPEN ROAD MEDIA

MYSTERIOUSPRESS.COM

Otto Penzler, owner of the Mysterious Bookshop in Manhattan, founded the Mysterious Press in 1975. Penzler quickly became known for his outstanding selection of mystery, crime, and suspense books, both from his imprint and in his store. The imprint was devoted to printing the best books in these genres, using fine paper and top dust-jacket artists, as well as offering many limited, signed editions.

Now the Mysterious Press has gone digital, publishing ebooks through **MysteriousPress.com**.

MysteriousPress.com offers readers essential noir and suspense fiction, hard-boiled crime novels, and the latest thrillers from both debut authors and mystery masters. Discover classics and new voices, all from one legendary source.

FIND OUT MORE AT

WWW.MYSTERIOUSPRESS.COM

FOLLOW US:

@emysteries and Facebook.com/MysteriousPressCom

MysteriousPress.com is one of a select group of publishing partners of Open Road Integrated Media, Inc.

THe MySTeRlOUS BOOKSHOP, founded in 1979, is located in Manhattan's Tribeca neighborhood. It is the oldest and largest mystery-specialty bookstore in America.

The shop stocks the finest selection of new mystery hardcovers, paperbacks, and periodicals. It also features a superb collection of signed modern first editions, rare and collectable works, and Sherlock Holmes titles. The bookshop issues a free monthly newsletter highlighting its book clubs, new releases, events, and recently acquired books.

58 Warren Street
info@mysteriousbookshop.com
(212) 587-1011
Monday through Saturday
11:00 a.m. to 7:00 p.m.

FIND OUT MORe AT:

www.mysteriousbookshop.com

FOLLOW US:

@TheMysterious and Facebook.com/MysteriousBookshop

OPEN ROAD

INTEGRATED MEDIA

Find a full list of our authors and
titles at www.openroadmedia.com

FOLLOW US
@OpenRoadMedia